SIR HARRY HOTSPUR
OF HUMBLETHWAITE

Anthony Trollope 1815-1882

Cover Painting:

"A Young Man at His Window" by Gustave Caillebotte, 1875.

Cover Design Copyright © 2009 by Vera Nazarian

ISBN-13: 978-1-60762-018-1
ISBN-10: 1-60762-018-9

First Publication: 1871

Reprint Trade Paperback Edition

January 2009

A Publication of
Norilana Books
P. O. Box 2188
Winnetka, CA 91396
www.norilana.com

Printed in the United States of America

Sir Harry Hotspur of Humblethwaite

Norilana Books
Classics

www.norilana.com

Sir Harry Hotspur of Humblethwaite

ଔଈୡଽ

Anthony Trollope

ଔଈୡଽ

Contents

Chapter I.

Sir Harry Hotspur.

Sir Harry Hotspur of Humblethwaite was a mighty person in Cumberland, and one who well understood of what nature were the duties, and of what sort the magnificence, which his position as a great English commoner required of him. He had twenty thousand a year derived from land. His forefathers had owned the same property in Cumberland for nearly four centuries, and an estate nearly as large in Durham for more than a century and a half. He had married an earl's daughter, and had always lived among men and women not only of high rank, but also of high character. He had kept race-horses when he was young, as noblemen and gentlemen then did keep them, with no view to profit, calculating fairly their cost as a part of his annual outlay, and thinking that it was the proper thing to do for the improvement of horses and for the amusement of the people. He had been in Parliament, but had made no figure there, and had given it up. He still kept his house in Bruton Street, and always spent a month or two in London. But the life that he led was led at Humblethwaite, and there he was a great man, with a great domain around him,—with many tenants, with a world of dependants among whom he spent his wealth freely, saving little, but lavishing nothing that was not his own to lavish,—understanding that his enjoyment was to come from the comfort and respect of others, for whose welfare, as he understood it, the good things of this world had been bestowed upon him. He was a proud man, with but few intimacies,—with a few dear friendships which were the solace of his life,—altogether gracious in his speech, if it were not for an apparent bashfulness among strangers; never assuming aught, deferring much to others outwardly, and showing his pride chiefly by a certain impalpable *noli me tangere*, which just sufficed to make itself felt and obeyed at the first approach of any personal freedom. He was a handsome man,—if an old man near to seventy may be handsome,—with grey hair, and bright, keen eyes, and arched eyebrows, with a well-cut eagle nose, and a small mouth, and a short dimpled chin. He was under the middle height, but nevertheless commanded attention by his appearance. He wore no beard save a slight grey whisker, which was cut away before it reached his chin. He was strongly made, but not stout, and was hale and active for his age.

Such was Sir Harry Hotspur of Humblethwaite. The account of Lady Elizabeth, his wife, may be much shorter. She was known,—where she was known,—simply as Sir Harry's wife. He indeed was one of those men of whom it may be said that everything appertaining to them takes its importance from the fact of its being theirs. Lady Elizabeth was a good woman, a good wife, and a good mother, and was twenty years younger than her husband. He had been forty-five years old when he had married her, and she, even yet, had not forgotten the deference which was due to his age.

Two years before the time at which our story will begin, a great sorrow, an absolutely crushing grief, had fallen upon the House of Humblethwaite. An only son had died just as he had reached his majority. When the day came on which all Humblethwaite and the surrounding villages were to have been told to rejoice and make merry because another man of the

Hotspurs was ready to take the reins of the house as soon as his father should have been gathered to his fathers, the poor lad lay a-dying, while his mother ministered by his bedside, and the Baronet was told by the physician—who had been brought from London—that there was no longer for him any hope that he should leave a male heir at Humblethwaite to inherit his name and his honours.

For months it was thought that Lady Elizabeth would follow her boy. Sir Harry bore the blow bravely, though none who do not understand the system well can conceive how the natural grief of the father was increased by the disappointment which had fallen upon the head of the house. But the old man bore it well, making but few audible moans, shedding no tears, altering in very little the habits of life; still spending money, because it was good for others that it should be spent, and only speaking of his son when it was necessary for him to allude to those altered arrangements as to the family property which it was necessary that he should make. But still he was a changed man, as those perceived who watched him closest. Cloudesdale the butler knew well in what he was changed, as did old Hesketh the groom, and Gilsby the gamekeeper. He had never been given to much talk, but was now more silent than of yore. Of horses, dogs, and game there was no longer any mention whatever made by the Baronet. He was still constant with Mr. Lanesby, the steward, because it was his duty to know everything that was done on the property; but even Mr. Lanesby would acknowledge that, as to actual improvements,—the commencement of new work in the hope of future returns, the Baronet was not at all the man he had been. How was it possible that he should be the man he had been when his life was so nearly gone, and that other life had gone also, which was to have been the renewal and continuation of his own?

When the blow fell, it became Sir Harry's imperative duty to make up his mind what he would do with his property. As regarded the two estates, they were now absolutely, every acre of them, at his own disposal. He had one child left him, a daughter,—in whom, it is hoped, the reader may be induced to take some interest, and with her to feel some sympathy, for she will be the person with whom the details of this little story must most be concerned; and he had a male heir, who must needs inherit the title of the family, one George Hotspur,—not a nephew, for Sir Harry had never had a brother, but the son of a first cousin who had not himself been much esteemed at Humblethwaite.

Now Sir Harry was a man who, in such a condition as this in which he was now placed, would mainly be guided by his ideas of duty. For a month or two he said not a word to any one, not even to his own lawyer, though he himself had made a will, a temporary will, duly witnessed by Mr. Lanesby and another, so that the ownership of the property should not be adjusted simply by the chance direction of law in the event of his own sudden demise; but his mind was doubtless much burdened with the subject. How should he discharge this fresh responsibility which now rested on him? While his boy had lived, the responsibility of his property had had nothing for him but charms. All was to go to the young Harry,—all, as a matter of course; and it was only necessary for him to take care that every acre should descend to his heir not only unimpaired by him in value, but also somewhat increased. Provision for his widow and for his girl had already been made before he had ventured on matrimony,— provision sufficient for many girls had Fortune so far favoured him. But that an eldest son should have all the family land,— one, though as many sons should have been given to him as to Priam,—and that that one should have it unencumbered, as he had had it from his father,—this was to him the very law of his being. And he would have taught that son, had already begun to teach him when the great blow came, that all this was to be given to him, not that he might put it into his own belly, or wear it on his own back, or even spend it as he might list himself, but that he might so live as to do his part in maintaining that order of gentlehood in England, by which England had become—so thought Sir Harry—the proudest and the greatest and the justest of nations.

But now he had no son, and yet the duty remained to him of maintaining his order. It would perhaps have been better for him, it would certainly have been easier, had some settlement or family entail fixed all things for him. Those who knew him well personally, but did not know the affairs of his family, declared among themselves that Sir Harry would take care that the property went with the title. A marriage might be arranged. There could be nothing to object to a marriage between second cousins. At any rate Sir Harry Hotspur was certainly not the man to separate the property from the title. But they who knew the family, and especially that branch of the family from which George Hotspur came, declared that Sir Harry would never give his daughter to such a one as was this cousin. And if not his daughter, then neither would he give to such a scapegrace either Humblethwaite in Cumberland or Scarrowby in Durham. There did exist a party who said that Sir Harry would divide the property, but they who held such an opinion certainly knew very little of Sir Harry's social or political tenets. Any such division was the one thing which he surely would not effect.

When twelve months had passed after the death of Sir Harry's son, George Hotspur had been at Humblethwaite and had gone, and Sir Harry's will had been made. He had left everything to his daughter, and had only stipulated that her husband, should she marry, should take the name of Hotspur. He had decided, that should his daughter, as was probable, marry within his lifetime, he could then make what settlements he pleased, even to the changing of the tenor of his will, should he think fit to change it. Should he die and leave her still a spinster, he would trust to her in everything. Not being a man of mystery, he told his wife and his daughter what he had done,—and what he still thought that he possibly might do; and being also a man to whom any suspicion of injustice was odious, he desired his attorney to make known to George Hotspur what had been settled. And in order that this blow to Cousin George might be lightened,—Cousin George having in conversation acknowledged to a few debts,—an immediate present was made to him of four thousand pounds, and double that amount was assured to him at the Baronet's death.

The reader may be sure that the Baronet had heard many things respecting Cousin George which he did not like. To him personally it would have been infinitely preferable that the title and the estates should have gone together, than that his own daughter should be a great heiress. That her outlook into the world was fair and full of promise of prosperity either way, was clear enough. Twenty thousand a year would not be necessary to make her a happy woman. And then it was to him a manifest and a sacred religion that to no man or to no woman were appointed the high pinnacles of fortune simply that that man or that woman might enjoy them. They were to be held as thrones are held, for the benefit of the many. And in the disposition of this throne, the necessity of making which had fallen upon him from the loss of his own darling, he had brought himself to think—not of his daughter's happiness, or to the balance of which, in her possessing or not possessing the property, he could venture on no prophecy,—but of the welfare of all those who might measure their weal or woe from the manner in which the duties of this high place were administered. He would fain that there should still have been a Sir Harry or a Sir George Hotspur of Humblethwaite; but he found that his duty required him to make the other arrangement.

And yet he had liked the cousin, who indeed had many gifts to win liking both from men and women. Previously to the visit very little had been known personally of young George Hotspur at Humblethwaite. His father, also a George, had in early life quarrelled with the elder branch of the family, and had gone off with what money belonged to him, and had lived and died in Paris. The younger George had been educated abroad, and then had purchased a commission in a regiment of English cavalry. At the time when young Harry died it was only known of him at Humblethwaite that he had achieved a certain reputation in London, and that he had sold out of the army. He was talked of as a man who shot birds with precision. Pigeons he could shoot with wonderful dexterity,—which art was at Humblethwaite supposed to be much against him. But then he was equally successful with partridges and pheasants; and partly on account of such success, and partly probably because his manner was pleasant, he was known to be a welcome guest at houses in which men congregate to slaughter game. In this way he had a reputation, and one that was not altogether cause for reproach; but it had not previously recommended him to the notice of his cousin.

Just ten months after poor Harry's death he was asked, and went, to Humblethwaite. Probably at that moment the Baronet's mind was still somewhat in doubt. The wish of Lady Elizabeth had been clearly expressed to her husband to the effect that encouragement should be given to the young people to fall in love with each other. To this Sir Harry never assented; though there was a time,—and that time had not yet passed when George Hotspur reached Humblethwaite,—in which the Baronet was not altogether averse to the idea of the marriage. But when George left Humblethwaite the Baronet had made up his mind. Tidings had reached him, and he was afraid of the cousin. And other tidings had reached him also; or rather perhaps it would be truer to him to say that another idea had come to him. Of all the young men now rising in England there was no young man who more approved himself to Sir Harry's choice than did Lord Alfred Gresley, the second son of his old friend and political leader the Marquis of Milnthorp. Lord Alfred had but scanty fortune of his own, but was in Parliament and in office, and was doing well. All men said all good things of him. Then there was a word or two spoken between the Marquis and the Baronet, and just a word also with Lord Alfred himself. Lord Alfred had no objection to the name of Hotspur. This was in October, while George Hotspur was still declaring that Gilbsy knew nothing of getting up a head of game; and then Lord Alfred promised to come to Humblethwaite at Christmas. It was after this that George owned to a few debts. His confession on that score did him no harm. Sir Harry had made up his mind that day. Sir Harry had at that time learned a good deal of his cousin George's mode of life in London, and had already decided that this young man was not one whom it would be well to set upon the pinnacle.

And yet he had liked the young man, as did everybody. Lady Elizabeth had liked him much, and for a fortnight had gone on hoping that all difficulties might have solved themselves by the young man's marriage with her daughter. It need hardly be said that not a word one way or the other was spoken to Emily Hotspur; but it seemed to the mother that the young people, though there was no love-making, yet liked each other. Sir Harry at this time was up in London for a month or two, hearing tidings, seeing Lord Alfred, who was at his office; and on his return, that solution by family marriage was ordered to be for ever banished from the maternal bosom. Sir Harry said that it would not do.

Nevertheless, he was good to the young cousin, and when the time was drawing nigh for the young man's departure he spoke of a further visit. The coverts at Humblethwaite, such as they were, would always be at his service. This was a week before the cousin went; but by the coming of the day on which the cousin took his departure Sir Harry regretted that he had made that offer of future hospitality.

Chapter II.

Our Heroine.

"He has said nothing to her?" asked Sir Harry, anxiously, of his wife.

"I think not," replied Lady Elizabeth.

"Had he said anything that meant anything, she would have told you?"

"Certainly she would," said Lady Elizabeth.

Sir Harry knew his child, and was satisfied that no harm had been done; nevertheless, he wished that that further invitation had not been given. If this Christmas visitor that was to come to Humblethwaite could be successful, all would be right; but it had seemed to Sir Harry, during that last week of Cousin George's sojourn beneath his roof, there had been more of cousinly friendship between the cousins than had been salutary, seeing, as he had seen, that any closer connection was inexpedient. But he thought that he was sure that no great harm had been done. Had any word been spoken to his girl which she herself had taken as a declaration of love, she would certainly have told her mother. Sir Harry would no more doubt his daughter than he would his own honour. There were certain points and lines of duty clearly laid down for a girl so placed as was his daughter; and Sir Harry, though he could not have told whence the knowledge of these points and lines had come to his child, never for a moment doubted but that she knew them, and would obey them. To know and to obey such points of duty were a part of the inheritance of such a one as Emily Hotspur. Nevertheless, it might be possible that her fancy should be touched, and that she herself should know nothing of it,— nothing that she could confide even to a mother. Sir Harry understanding this, and having seen in these last days something as he thought of too close a cousinly friendship, was anxious that Lord Alfred should come and settle everything. If Lord Alfred should be successful, all danger would be at an end, and the cousin might come again and do what he liked with the coverts. Alas, alas! the cousin should never have been allowed to show his handsome, wicked face at Humblethwaite!

Emily Hotspur was a girl whom any father would have trusted; and let the reader understand this of her, that she was one in whom intentional deceit was impossible. Neither to her father nor to any one could she lie either in word or action. And all these lines and points of duty were well known to her, though she knew not, and had never asked herself, whence the lesson had come. Will it be too much to say, that they had formed a part of her breeding, and had been given to her with her blood? She understood well that from her, as heiress of the House of Humblethwaite, a double obedience was due to her father,—the obedience of a child added to that which was now required from her as the future transmitter of honours of the house. And yet no word had been said to her of the honours of the house; nor, indeed, had many words ever been said as to that other obedience. These lessons, when they have been well learned, have ever come without direct teaching.

But she knew more than this, and the knowledge had reached her in the same manner. Though she owed a great duty to her father, there was a limit to that duty, of which, unconsciously, she was well aware. When her mother told her that Lord Alfred was coming, having been instructed to do so by Sir Harry; and hinted, with a caress and a kiss, and a soft whisper, that Lord Alfred was one of whom Sir Harry approved greatly, and that if further approval could be bestowed Sir Harry would not be displeased, Emily as she returned her mother's embrace, felt that she had a possession of her own with which neither father nor mother might be allowed to interfere. It was for them, or rather for him, to say that a hand so weighted as was hers should not be given here or there; but it was not for them, not even for him, to say that her heart was to be given here, or to be given there. Let them put upon her what weight they might of family honours, and of family responsibility, that was her own property;—if not, perhaps, to be bestowed at her own pleasure, because of the pressure of that weight, still her own, and absolutely beyond the bestowal of any other.

Nevertheless, she declared to herself, and whispered to her mother, that she would be glad to welcome Lord Alfred. She had known him well when she was a child of twelve years old and he was already a young man in Parliament. Since those days she had met him more than once in London. She was now turned twenty, and he was something more than ten years her senior; but there was nothing against him, at any rate, on the score of age. Lord Alfred was admitted on every side to be still a young man; and though he had already been a lord of one Board or of another for the last four years, and had earned a reputation for working, he did not look like a man who would be more addicted to sitting at Boards than spending his time with young women. He was handsome, pleasant, good-humoured, and full of talk; had nothing about him of the official fogy; and was regarded by all his friends as a man who was just now fit to marry. "They say that he is such a good son, and such a good brother," said Lady Elizabeth, anxiously.

"Quite a Phoenix!" said Emily, laughing. Then Lady Elizabeth began to fear that she had said too much, and did not mention Lord Alfred's name for two days.

But Miss Hotspur had by that time resolved that Lord Alfred should have a fair chance. If she could teach herself to think that of all men walking the earth Lord Alfred was the best and the most divine, the nearest of all men to a god, how excellent a thing would it be! Her great responsibility as to the family burden would in that case already be acquitted with credit. The wishes of her father, which on such a subject were all but paramount, would be gratified; and she herself would then be placed almost beyond the hand of misfortune to hurt her. At any rate, the great and almost crushing difficulty of her life would so be solved. But the man must have enough in her eyes of that godlike glory to satisfy her that she had found in him one who would be almost a divinity, at any rate to her. Could he speak as that other man spoke? Could he look as that other one looked? Would there be in his eye such a depth of colour, in his voice such a sound of music, in his gait so divine a grace? For that other one, though she had looked into the brightness of the colour, though she had heard the sweetness of the music, though she had watched the elastic spring of the step, she cared nothing as regarded her heart—her heart, which was the one treasure of her own. No; she was sure of that. Of her one own great treasure, she was much too chary to give it away unasked, and too independent, as she told herself, to give it away unauthorized. The field was open to Lord Alfred; and, as her father wished it, Lord Alfred should be received with every favour. If she could find divinity, then she would bow before it readily.

Alas for Lord Alfred! We may all know that when she thought of it thus, there was but poor chance of success for Lord Alfred. Let him have what of the godlike he might, she would find but little of it there when she made her calculations and resolutions after such fashion as this. The man who becomes divine in a woman's eyes, has generally achieved his claim to celestial honours by sudden assault. And, alas! the qualities which carry him through it and give the halo to his head may after all be very ungodlike. Some such achievement had already fallen in the way of Cousin George; though had Cousin George and Lord Alfred been weighed in just scales, the divinity of the latter, such as it was, would have been found greatly to prevail. Indeed, it might perhaps have been difficult to lay hold of and bring forward as presentable for such office as that of a lover for such a girl any young man who should be less godlike than Cousin George. But he had gifts of simulation, which are valuable; and poor Emily Hotspur had not yet learned the housewife's trick of passing the web through her fingers, and of finding by the touch whether the fabric were of fine wool, or of shoddy made up with craft to look like wool of the finest.

We say that there was but small chance for Lord Alfred; nevertheless the lady was dutifully minded to give him all the chance that it was in her power to bestow. She did not tell herself that her father's hopes were vain. Of her preference for that other man she never told herself anything. She was not aware that it existed. She knew that he was handsome; she thought that he was clever. She knew that he had talked to her as no man had ever talked before. She was aware that he was her nearest relative beyond her father and mother, and that therefore she might be allowed to love him as a cousin. She told herself that he was a Hotspur, and that he must be the head of the Hotspurs when her father should be taken from them. She thought that he looked as a man should look who would have to carry such a dignity. But there was nothing more. No word had been said to her on the subject; but she was aware, because no word had been said, that it was not thought fitting that she should be her cousin's bride. She could not but know how great would be the advantage could the estates and the title be kept together. Even though he should inherit no acre of the land,— and she had been told by her father that such was his decision,— this Cousin George must become the head of the House of Hotspur; and to be head of the House of Hotspur was to her a much greater thing than to be the owner of Humblethwaite and Scarrowby. Gifts like the latter might be given to a mere girl, like herself,—were to be so given. But let any man living do what he might, George Hotspur must become the head and chief of the old House of Hotspur. Nevertheless, it was not for her to join the two things together, unless her father should see that it would be good for her to do so.

Emily Hotspur was very like her father, having that peculiar cast of countenance which had always characterized the family. She had the same arch in her eyebrows, indicating an aptitude for authority; the same well-formed nose, though with her the beak of the eagle was less prominent; the same short lip, and small mouth, and delicate dimpled chin. With both of them the lower part of the face was peculiarly short, and finely cut. With both of them the brow was high and broad, and the temples prominent. But the girl's eyes were blue, while those of the old man were brightly green. It was told of him that when a boy his eyes also had been blue. Her hair, which was very plentiful, was light in colour, but by no means flaxen. Her complexion was as clear as the finest porcelain; but there were ever roses in her cheeks, for she was strong by nature, and her health was perfect. She was somewhat short of stature, as were all the Hotspurs, and her feet and hands and ears were small and delicate. But though short, she seemed to lack nothing in symmetry, and certainly lacked nothing in strength. She could ride or walk the whole day, and had no feeling that such vigour of body was a possession of which a young lady should be ashamed. Such as she was, she was the acknowledged beauty of the county; and at Carlisle, where she showed herself at least once a year at the county ball, there was neither man nor woman, young nor old, who was not ready to say that Emily Hotspur was, among maidens, the glory of Cumberland.

Her life hitherto had been very quiet. There was the ball at Carlisle, which she had attended thrice; on the last occasion, because of her brother's death, she had been absent, and the family of the Hotspurs had been represented there only by the venison and game which had been sent from Humblethwaite.

Twice also she had spent the months of May and June in London; but it had not hitherto suited the tone of her father's character to send his daughter out into all the racket of a London season. She had gone to balls, and to the opera, and had ridden in the Park, and been seen at flower-shows; but she had not been so common in those places as to be known to the crowd. And, hitherto, neither in town or country, had her name been connected with that of any suitor for her hand. She was now twenty, and the reader will remember that in the twelve months last past, the House of Humblethwaite had been clouded with deep mourning.

The cousin was come and gone, and the Baronet hoped in his heart that there might be an end of him as far as Humblethwaite was concerned;—at any rate till his child should have given herself to a better lover. Tidings had been sent to Sir Harry during the last week of the young man's sojourn beneath his roof, which of all that had reached his ears were the worst. He had before heard of recklessness, of debt, of dissipation, of bad comrades. Now he heard of worse than these. If that which he now heard was true, there had been dishonour. But Sir Harry was a man who wanted ample evidence before he allowed his judgment to actuate his conduct, and in this case the evidence was far from ample. He did not stint his hospitality to the future baronet, but he failed to repeat that promise of a future welcome which had already been given, and which had been thankfully accepted. But a man knows that such an offer of renewed hospitality should be repeated at the moment of departure, and George Hotspur, as he was taken away to the nearest station in his cousin's carriage, was quite aware that Sir Harry did not then desire that the visit should be repeated.

Lord Alfred was to be at Humblethwaite on Christmas Eve. The emergencies of the Board at which he sat would not allow of an earlier absence from London. He was a man who shirked no official duty, and was afraid of no amount of work; and though he knew how great was the prize before him, he refused to leave his Board before the day had come at which his Board must necessarily dispense with his services. Between him and his father there had been no reticence, and it was clearly understood by him that he was to go down and win twenty thousand a year and the prettiest girl in Cumberland, if his own capacity that way, joined to all the favour of the girl's father and mother, would enable him to attain success. To Emily not a word more had been said on the subject than those which have been already narrated as having been spoken by the mother to the daughter. With all his authority, with all his love for his only remaining child, with all his consciousness of the terrible importance of the matter at issue, Sir Harry could not bring himself to suggest to his daughter that it would be well for her to fall in love with the guest who was coming to them. But to Lady Elizabeth he said very much. He had quite made up his mind that the thing would be good, and, having done so, he was very anxious that the arrangement should be made. It was natural that this girl of his should learn to love some youth; and how terrible was the danger of her loving amiss, when so much depended on her loving wisely! The whole fate of the House of Hotspur was in her hands,—to do with it as she thought fit! Sir Harry trembled as he reflected what would be the result were she to come to him some day and ask his favour for a suitor wholly unfitted to bear the name of Hotspur, and to sit on the throne of Humblethwaite and Scarrowby.

"Is she pleased that he is coming?" he said to his wife, the evening before the arrival of their guest.

"Certainly she is pleased. She knows that we both like him."

"I remember when she used to talk about him—often," said Sir Harry.

"That was when she was a child."

"But a year or two ago," said Sir Harry.

"Three or four years, perhaps; and with her that is a long time. It is not likely that she should talk much of him now. Of course she knows what it is that we wish."

"Does she think about her cousin at all?" he said some hours afterwards.

"Yes, she thinks of him. That is only natural, you know."

"It would be unnatural that she should think of him much."

"I do not see that," said the mother, keen to defend her daughter from what might seem to be an implied reproach. "George Hotspur is a man who will make himself thought of wherever he goes. He is clever, and very amusing;—there is no denying that. And then he has the Hotspur look all over."

"I wish he had never set his foot within the house," said the father.

"My dear, there is no such danger as you think," said Lady Elizabeth. "Emily is not a girl prone to fall in love at a moment's notice because a man is good-looking and amusing;— and certainly not with the conviction which she must have that her doing so would greatly grieve you." Sir Harry believed in his daughter, and said no more; but he thoroughly wished that Lord Alfred's wedding-day was fixed.

"Mamma," said Emily, on the following day, "won't Lord Alfred be very dull?"

"I hope not, my dear."

"What is he to do, with nobody else here to amuse him?"

"The Crutchleys are coming on the 27th."

Now Mr. and Mrs. Crutchley were, as Emily thought, very ordinary people, and quite unlikely to afford amusement to Lord Alfred. Mr. Crutchley was an old gentleman of county standing, and with property in the county, living in a large dull red house in Penrith, of whom Sir Harry thought a good deal, because he was a gentleman who happened to have had great-grandfathers and great-grandmothers. But he was quite as old as

Sir Harry, and Mrs. Crutchley was a great deal older than Lady Elizabeth.

"What will Lord Alfred have to say to Mrs. Crutchley, mamma?"

"What do people in society always have to say to each other? And the Lathebys are coming here to dine to-morrow, and will come again, I don't doubt, on the 27th."

Mr. Latheby was the young Vicar of Humblethwaite, and Mrs. Latheby was a very pretty young bride whom he had just married.

"And then Lord Alfred shoots," continued Lady Elizabeth.

"Cousin George said that the shooting wasn't worth going after," said Emily, smiling. "Mamma, I fear it will be a failure." This made Lady Elizabeth unhappy, as she thought that more was meant than was really said. But she did not confide her fears to her husband.

Chapter III.

Lord Alfred's Courtship.

The Hall, as the great house at Humblethwaite was called, consisted in truth of various edifices added one to another at various periods; but the result was this, that no more picturesque mansion could be found in any part of England than the Hall at Humblethwaite. The oldest portion of it was said to be of the time of Henry VII.; but it may perhaps be doubted whether the set of rooms with lattice windows looking out on to the bowling-green, each window from beneath its own gable, was so old as the date assigned to it. It is strange how little authority can usually be found in family records to verify such statements. It was known that Humblethwaite and the surrounding manors had been given to, or in some fashion purchased by, a certain Harry Hotspur, who also in his day had been a knight, when Church lands were changing hands under Henry VIII. And there was authority to prove that that Sir Harry had done something towards making a home for himself on the spot; but whether those very gables were a portion of the building which the monks of St. Humble had raised for themselves in the preceding reign, may probably be doubted. That there were fragments of masonry, and parts of old timber, remaining from the monastery was probably true enough. The great body of the old house, as it now stood, had been built in the time of Charles II., and there was the date in the brickwork still conspicuous on the wall looking into the court. The hall and front door as it now stood, very prominent but quite at the end of the house, had been erected in the reign of Queen Anne, and the modern drawing-rooms with the best bedrooms over them, projecting far out into the modern gardens, had been added by the present baronet's father. The house was entirely of brick, and the old windows,—not the very oldest, the reader will understand, but those of the Caroline age,—were built with strong stone mullions, and were longer than they were deep, beauty of architecture having in those days been more regarded than light. Who does not know such windows, and has not declared to himself often how sad a thing it is that sanitary or scientific calculations should have banished the like of them from our houses? Two large oriel windows coming almost to the ground, and going up almost to the ceilings, adorned the dining-room and the library. From the drawing-rooms modern windows, opening on to a terrace, led into the garden.

You entered the mansion by a court that was enclosed on two sides altogether, and on the two others partially. Facing you, as you drove in, was the body of the building, with the huge porch projecting on the right so as to give the appearance of a portion of the house standing out on that side. On the left was that old mythic Tudor remnant of the monastery, of which the back wall seen from the court was pierced only with a small window here and there, and was covered with ivy. Those lattice windows, from which Emily Hotspur loved to think that the monks of old had looked into their trim gardens, now looked on to a bowling-green which was kept very trim in honour of the holy personages who were supposed to have played there four centuries ago. Then, at the end of this old building, there had been erected kitchens, servants' offices, and various rooms, which turned the corner of the court in front, so that only one corner had, as it were, been left for ingress and egress. But the court itself was large, and in the middle of it there stood an old stone ornamental structure, usually called the fountain, but quite ignorant of water, loaded with griffins and satyrs and mermaids with ample busts, all overgrown with a green damp growth, which was scraped off by the joint efforts of the gardener and mason once perhaps in every five years.

It often seems that the beauty of architecture is accidental. A great man goes to work with great means on a great pile, and makes a great failure. The world perceives that grace and beauty have escaped him, and that even magnificence has been hardly achieved. Then there grows up beneath various unknown hands a complication of stones and brick to the arrangement of which no great thought seems to have been given; and, lo, there is a thing so perfect in its glory that he who looks at it declares that nothing could be taken away and nothing added without injury and sacrilege and disgrace. So it had been, or rather so it was now, with the Hall at Humblethwaite. No rule ever made for the guidance of an artist had been kept. The parts were out of proportion. No two parts seemed to fit each other. Put it all on paper, and it was an absurdity. The huge hall and porch added on by the builder of Queen Anne's time, at the very extremity of the house, were almost a monstrosity. The passages and staircases, and internal arrangements, were simply ridiculous. But there was not a portion of the whole interior that did not charm; nor was there a corner of the exterior, nor a yard of an outside wall, that was not in itself eminently beautiful.

Lord Alfred Gresley, as he was driven into the court in the early dusk of a winter evening, having passed through a mile and a half of such park scenery as only Cumberland and Westmoreland can show, was fully alive to the glories of the place. Humblethwaite did not lie among the lakes,—was, indeed, full ten miles to the north of Keswick; but it was so placed that it enjoyed the beauty and the luxury of mountains and rivers, without the roughness of unmanageable rocks, or the sterility and dampness of moorland. Of rocky fragments, indeed, peeping out through the close turf, and here and there coming forth boldly so as to break the park into little depths, with now and again a real ravine, there were plenty. And there ran right across the park, passing so near the Hall as to require a stone bridge in the very flower-garden, the Caldbeck, as bright and swift a stream as ever took away the water from neighbouring mountains. And to the south of Humblethwaite there stood the huge Skiddaw, and Saddleback with its long gaunt ridge; while to the west, Brockleband Fell seemed to encircle the domain. Lord Alfred, as he was driven up through the old trees, and saw the deer peering at him from the knolls and broken fragments of stone, felt that he need not envy his elder brother if only his lines might fall to him in this very pleasant place.

He had known Humblethwaite before; and, irrespective of all its beauties, and of the wealth of the Hotspurs, was quite willing to fall in love with Emily Hotspur. That a man with such dainties offered to him should not become greedy, that there should be no touch of avarice when such wealth was shown to him, is almost more than we may dare to assert. But Lord Alfred was a man not specially given to covetousness. He had recognized it as his duty as a man not to seek for these things unless he could in truth love the woman who held them in her hands to give. But as he looked round him through the gloaming of the evening, he thought that he remembered that Emily Hotspur was all that was loveable.

But, reader, we must not linger long over Lord Alfred's love. A few words as to the father, a few as to the daughter, and a few also as to the old house where they dwelt together, it has been necessary to say; but this little love story of Lord Alfred's,—if it ever was a love story,—must be told very shortly.

He remained five weeks at Humblethwaite, and showed himself willing to receive amusement from old Mrs. Crutchley and from young Mrs. Latheby. The shooting was quite good enough for him, and he won golden opinions from every one about the place. He made himself acquainted with the whole history of the house, and was prepared to prove to demonstration that Henry VII.'s monks had looked out of those very windows, and had played at bowls on that very green. Emily became fond of him after a fashion, but he failed to assume any aspect of divinity in her eyes.

Of the thing to be done, neither father nor mother said a word to the girl; and she, though she knew so well that the doing of it was intended, said not a word to her mother. Had Lady Elizabeth known how to speak, had she dared to be free with her own child, Emily would soon have told her that there was no chance for Lord Alfred. And Lady Elizabeth would have believed her. Nay, Lady Elizabeth, though she could not speak, had the woman's instinct, which almost assured her that the match would never be made. Sir Harry, on the other side, thought that things went prosperously; and his wife did not dare to undeceive him. He saw the young people together, and thought that he saw that Emily was kind. He did not know that this frank kindness was incompatible with love in such a maiden's ways. As for Emily herself, she knew that it must come. She knew that she could not prevent it. A slight hint or two she did give, or thought she gave, but they were too fine, too impalpable to be of avail.

Lord Alfred spoke nothing of love till he made his offer in form. At last he was not hopeful himself. He had found it impossible to speak to this girl of love. She had been gracious with him, and almost intimate, and yet it had been impossible. He thought of himself that he was dull, stupid, lethargic, and miserably undemonstrative. But the truth was that there was nothing for him to demonstrate. He had come there to do a stroke of business, and he could not throw into this business a spark of that fire which would have been kindled by such sympathy had it existed. There are men who can raise such sparks, the pretence of fire, where there is no heat at all;—false, fraudulent men; but he was not such an one. Nevertheless he went on with his business.

"Miss Hotspur," he said to her one morning between breakfast and lunch, when, as usual, opportunity had been given him to be alone with her, "I have something to say to you, which I hope at any rate it will not make you angry to hear."

"I am sure you will say nothing to make me angry," she replied.

"I have already spoken to your father, and I have his permission. I may say more. He assures me that he hopes I may succeed." He paused a moment, but she remained quite tranquil. He watched her, and could see that the delicate pink on her cheek was a little heightened, and that a streak of colour showed itself on her fair brow; but there was nothing in her manner to give him either promise of success or assurance of failure. "You will know what I mean?"

"Yes, I know," she said, almost in a whisper.

"And may I hope? To say that I love you dearly seems to be saying what must be a matter of course."

"I do not see that at all," she replied with spirit.

"I do love you very dearly. If I may be allowed to think that you will be my wife, I shall be the happiest man in England. I know how great is the honour which I seek, how immense in every way is the gift which I ask you to give me. Can you love me?"

"No," she said, again dropping her voice to a whisper.

"Is that all the answer, Miss Hotspur?"

"What should I say? How ought I to answer you? If I could say it without seeming to be unkind, indeed, indeed, I would do so."

"Perhaps I have been abrupt."

"It is not that. When you ask me—to—to—love you, of course I know what you mean. Should I not speak the truth at once?"

"Must this be for always?"

"For always," she replied. And then it was over.

He did not himself press his suit further, though he remained at Humblethwaite for three days after this interview.

Before lunch on that day the story had been told by Emily to her mother, and by Lord Alfred to Sir Harry. Lady Elizabeth knew well enough that the story would never have to be told in another way. Sir Harry by no means so easily gave up his enterprise. He proposed to Lord Alfred that Emily should be asked to reconsider her verdict. With his wife he was very round, saying that an answer given so curtly should go for nothing, and that the girl must be taught her duty. With Emily herself he was less urgent, less authoritative, and indeed at last somewhat suppliant. He explained to her how excellent would be the marriage; how it would settle this terrible responsibility which now lay on his shoulders with so heavy a weight; how glorious would be her position; and how the Hotspurs would still live as a great family could she bring herself to be obedient. And he said very much in praise of Lord Alfred, pointing out how good a man he was, how moral, how diligent, how safe, how clever,—how sure, with the assistance of the means which she would give him, to be one of the notable men of the country. But she never yielded an inch. She said very little,—answered him hardly a word, standing close to him, holding by his arm and his hand. There was the fact, that she would not have the man, would not have the man now or ever, certainly would not have him; and Sir Harry, let him struggle as he might, and talk his best, could not keep himself from giving absolute credit to her assurance.

The visit was prolonged for three days, and then Lord Alfred left Humblethwaite Hall, with less appreciation of all its beauties than he had felt as he was first being driven up to the Hall doors. When he went, Sir Harry could only bid God bless him, and assure him that, should he ever choose to try his fortune again, he should have all the aid which a father could give him.

"It would be useless," said Lord Alfred; "she knows her own mind too well."

And so he went his way.

Chapter IV.

Vacillation.

When the spring-time came, Sir Harry Hotspur with his wife and daughter, went up to London. During the last season the house in Bruton Street had been empty. He and his wife were then mourning their lost son, and there was no place for the gaiety of London in their lives. Sir Harry was still thinking of his great loss. He was always thinking of the boy who was gone, who had been the apple of his eye, his one great treasure, the only human being in the world whose superior importance to his own he had been ready, in his heart of hearts, to admit; but it was needful that the outer signs of sorrow should be laid aside, and Emily Hotspur was taken up to London, in order that she might be suited with a husband. That, in truth, was the reason of their going. Neither Sir Harry nor Lady Elizabeth would have cared to leave Cumberland had there been no such cause. They would have been altogether content to remain at home had Emily been obedient enough in the winter to accept the hand of the suitor proposed for her.

The house was opened in Bruton Street, and Lord Alfred came to see them. So also did Cousin George. There was no reason why Cousin George should not come. Indeed, had he not done so, he must have been the most ungracious of cousins. He came, and found Lady Elizabeth and Emily at home. Emily told him that they were always there to receive visitors on Sundays after morning church, and then he came again. She had made no such communication to Lord Alfred, but then perhaps it would have been hardly natural that she should have done so. Lady Elizabeth, in a note which she had occasion to write to Lord Alfred, did tell him of her custom on a Sunday afternoon; but Lord Alfred took no such immediate advantage of the offer as did Cousin George.

As regarded the outward appearance of their life, the Hotspurs were gayer this May than they had been heretofore when living in London. There were dinner-parties, whereas in previous times there had only been dinners at which a few friends might join them;—and there was to be a ball. There was a box at the Opera, and there were horses for the Park, and there was an understanding that the dealings with Madame Milvodi, the milliner, were to be as unlimited as the occasion demanded. It was perceived by every one that Miss Hotspur was to be settled in life. Not a few knew the story of Lord Alfred. Every one knew the facts of the property and Emily's position as heiress, though every one probably did not know that it was still in Sir Harry's power to leave every acre of the property to whom he pleased. Emily understood it all herself. There lay upon her that terrible responsibility of doing her best with the Hotspur interests. To her the death of her brother had at the time been the blackest of misfortunes, and it was not the less so now as she thought of her own position. She had been steady enough as to the refusal of Lord Alfred, knowing well enough that she cared nothing for him. But there had since come upon her moments almost of regret that she should have been unable to accept him. It would have been so easy a way of escape from all her troubles without the assistance of Madame Milvodi, and the opera-box, and the Park horses! At the time she had her own ideas about another man, but her ideas were not such as to make her think that any further work with Madame Milvodi and the opera-box would be unnecessary.

Then came the question of asking Cousin George to the house. He had already been told to come on Sundays, and on the very next Sunday had been there. He had given no cause of offence at Humblethwaite, and Lady Elizabeth was of opinion that he should be asked to dinner. If he were not asked, the very omission would show that they were afraid of him. Lady Elizabeth did not exactly explain this to her husband,—did not accurately know that such was her fear; but Sir Harry understood her feelings, and yielded. Let Cousin George be asked to dinner.

Sir Harry at this time was vacillating with more of weakness than would have been expected from a man who had generally been so firm in the affairs of his life. He had been quite clear about George Hotspur, when those inquiries of his were first made, and when his mind had first accepted the notion of Lord Alfred as his chosen son-in-law. But now he was again at sea. He was so conscious of the importance of his daughter's case, that he could not bring himself to be at ease, and to allow himself to expect that the girl would, in the ordinary course of nature, dispose of her young heart not to her own injury, as might reasonably be hoped from her temperament, her character, and her education. He could not protect himself from daily and hourly thought about it. Her marriage was not as the marriage of other girls. The house of Hotspur, which had lived and prospered for so many centuries, was to live and prosper through her; or rather mainly through the man whom she should choose as her husband. The girl was all-important now, but when she should have once disposed of herself her importance would be almost at an end. Sir Harry had in the recess of his mind almost a conviction that, although the thing was of such utmost moment, it would be better for him, better for them all, better for the Hotspurs, that the matter should be allowed to arrange itself than that there should be any special judgment used in selection. He almost believed that his girl should be left to herself, as are other girls. But the thing was of such moment that he could not save himself from having it always before his eyes.

And yet he knew not what to do; nor was there any aid forthcoming from Lady Elizabeth. He had tried his hand at the choice of a proper husband, and his daughter would have none of the man so chosen. So he had brought her up to London, and thrown her as it were upon the market. Let Madame Milvodi and the opera-box and the Park horses do what they could for her. Of course a watch should be kept on her;—not from doubt of her excellence, but because the thing to be disposed of was so all-important, and the girl's mode of disposing of it might, without disgrace or fault on her part, be so vitally prejudicial to the family!

For, let it be remembered, no curled darling of an eldest son would suit the exigencies of the case, unless such eldest son were willing altogether to merge the claims of his own family, and to make himself by name and purpose a Hotspur. Were his child to present to him as his son-in-law some heir to a noble house, some future earl, say even a duke in embryo, all that would be as nothing to Sir Harry. It was not his ambition to see his daughter a duchess. He wanted no name, or place, or dominion for any Hotspur greater or higher or more noble than those which the Hotspurs claimed and could maintain for themselves. To have Humblethwaite and Scarrowby lost amidst the vast appanages and domains of some titled family, whose gorgeous glories were new and paltry in comparison with the mellow honours of his own house, would to him have been a ruin to all his hopes. There might, indeed, be some arrangement as to the second son proceeding from such a marriage,—as to a future chance Hotspur; but the claims of the Hotspurs were, he thought, too high and too holy for such future chance; and in such case, for one generation at least, the Hotspurs would be in abeyance. No: it was not that which he desired. That would not suffice for him. The son-in-law that he desired should be well born, a perfect gentleman, with belongings of whom he and his child might be proud; but he should be one who should be content to rest his claims to material prosperity and personal position on the name and wealth that he would obtain with his wife. Lord Alfred had been the very man; but then his girl would have none of Lord Alfred! Eldest sons there might be in plenty ready to take such a bride; and were some eldest son to come to him and ask for his daughter's hand, some eldest son who would do so almost with a right to claim it if the girl's consent were gained, how could he refuse? And yet to leave a Hotspur behind him living at Humblethwaite, and Hotspurs who should follow that Hotspur, was all in all to him.

Might he venture to think once again of Cousin George? Cousin George was there, coming to the house, and his wife was telling him that it was incumbent on them to ask the young man to dinner. It was incumbent on them, unless they meant to let him know that he was to be regarded absolutely as a stranger,— as one whom they had taken up for a while, and now chose to drop again. A very ugly story had reached Sir Harry's ears about Cousin George. It was said that he had twice borrowed money from the money-lenders on his commission, passing some document for security of its value which was no security, and that he had barely escaped detection, the two Jews knowing that the commission would be forfeited altogether if the fraud were brought to light. The commission had been sold, and the proceeds divided between the Jews, with certain remaining claims to them on Cousin George's personal estate. Such had been the story which in a vague way had reached Sir Harry's ears. It is not easily that such a man as Sir Harry can learn the details of a disreputable cousin's life. Among all his old friends he had none more dear to him than Lord Milnthorp; and among his younger friends none more intimate than Lord Burton, the eldest son of Lord Milnthorp, Lord Alfred's brother. Lord Burton had told him the story, telling him at the same time that he could not vouch for its truth. "Upon my word, I don't know," said Lord Burton, when interrogated again. "I think if I were you

I would regard it as though I had never heard it. Of course, he was in debt."

"That is altogether another thing," said Sir Harry.

"Altogether! I think that probably he did pawn his commission. That is bad, but it isn't so very bad. As for the other charge against him, I doubt it." So said Lord Burton, and Sir Harry determined that the accusation should go for nothing.

But his own child, his only child, the transmitter of all the great things that fortune had given to him; she, in whose hands were to lie the glories of Humblethwaite and Scarrowby; she, who had the giving away of the honour of their ancient family,—could she be trusted to one of whom it must be admitted that all his early life had been disreputable, even if the world's lenient judgment in such matters should fail to stigmatize it as dishonourable? In other respects, however, he was so manifestly the man to whom his daughter ought to be given in marriage! By such arrangement would the title and the property be kept together,—and by no other which Sir Harry could now make, for his word had been given to his daughter that she was to be his heiress. Let him make what arrangements he might, this Cousin George, at his death, would be the head of the family. Every "Peerage" that was printed would tell the old story to all the world. By certain courtesies of the law of descent his future heirs would be Hotspurs were his daughter married to Lord Alfred or the like; but the children of such a marriage would not be Hotspurs in very truth, nor by any courtesy of law, or even by any kindness of the Minister or Sovereign, could the child of such a union become the baronet, the Sir Harry of the day, the head of the family. The position was one which no Sovereign and no Minister could achieve, or touch, or bestow. It was his, beyond the power of any earthly potentate to deprive him of it, and would have been transmitted by him to a son with as absolute security. But—alas! alas!

Sir Harry gave no indication that he thought it expedient to change his mind on the subject. When Lady Elizabeth proposed that Cousin George should be asked to dinner, he frowned and looked black as he acceded; but, in truth, he vacillated. The allurements on that side were so great that he could not altogether force upon himself the duty of throwing them from him. He knew that Cousin George was no fitting husband for his girl, that he was a man to whom he would not have thought of giving her, had her happiness been his only object. And he did not think of so bestowing her now. He became uneasy when he remembered the danger. He was unhappy as he remembered how amusing, how handsome, how attractive was Cousin George. He feared that Emily might like him!—by no means hoped it. And yet he vacillated, and allowed Cousin George to come to the house, only because Cousin George must become, on his death, the head of the Hotspurs.

Cousin George came on one Sunday, came on another Sunday, dined at the house, and was of course asked to the ball. But Lady Elizabeth had so arranged her little affairs that when Cousin George left Bruton Street on the evening of the dinner party he and Emily had never been for two minutes alone together since the family had come up to London. Lady Elizabeth herself liked Cousin George, and, had an edict to that effect been pronounced by her husband, would have left them alone together with great maternal satisfaction. But she had been told that it was not to be so, and therefore the young people had never been allowed to have opportunities. Lady Elizabeth in her very quiet way knew how to do the work of the world that was allotted to her. There had been other balls, and there had been ridings in the Park, and all the chances of life which young men, and sometimes young women also, know so well how to use; but hitherto Cousin George had kept, or had been constrained to keep, his distance.

"I want to know, Mamma," said Emily Hotspur, the day before the ball, "whether Cousin George is a black sheep or a white sheep?"

"What do you mean, my dear, by asking such a question as that?"

"I don't like black sheep. I don't see why young men are to be allowed to be black sheep; but yet you know they are."

"How can it be helped?"

"People should not notice them, Mamma."

"My dear, it is a most difficult question,—quite beyond me, and I am sure beyond you. A sheep needn't be black always because he has not always been quite white; and then you know the black lambs are just as dear to their mother as the white."

"Dearer, I think."

"I quite agree with you, Emily, that in general society black sheep should be avoided."

"Then they shouldn't be allowed to come in," said Emily. Lady Elizabeth knew from this that there was danger, but the danger was not of a kind which enabled her specially to consult Sir Harry.

Chapter V.

George Hotspur.

A little must now be told to the reader of Cousin George and the ways of his life. As Lady Elizabeth had said to her daughter, that question of admitting black sheep into society, or of refusing them admittance, is very difficult. In the first place, whose eyes are good enough to know whether in truth a sheep be black or not? And then is it not the fact that some little amount of shade in the fleece of male sheep is considered, if not absolutely desirable, at any rate quite pardonable? A male sheep with a fleece as white as that of a ewe-lamb,—is he not considered to be, among muttons, somewhat insipid? It was of this taste which Pope was conscious when he declared that every woman was at heart a rake. And so it comes to pass that very black sheep indeed are admitted into society, till at last anxious fathers and more anxious mothers begin to be aware that their young ones are turned out to graze among ravenous wolves. This, however, must be admitted, that lambs when so treated acquire a courage which tends to enable them to hold their own, even amidst wolfish dangers.

Cousin George, if not a ravenous wolf, was at any rate a very black sheep indeed. In our anxiety to know the truth of him

it must not be said that he was absolutely a wolf,—not as yet,—
because in his career he had not as yet made premeditated
attempts to devour prey. But in the process of delivering himself
up to be devoured by others, he had done things which if known
of any sheep should prevent that sheep from being received into
a decent flock. There had been that little trouble about his
commission, in which, although he had not intended to cheat
either Jew, he had done that which the world would have called
cheating had the world known it. As for getting goods from
tradesmen without any hope or thought of paying for them, that
with him was so much a thing of custom,—as indeed it was also
with them,—that he was almost to be excused for considering it
the normal condition of life for a man in his position. To gamble
and lose money had come to him quite naturally at a very early
age. There had now come upon him an idea that he might turn
the tables, that in all gambling transactions some one must win,
and that as he had lost much, so possibly might he now win
more. He had not quite yet reached that point in his education at
which the gambler learns that the ready way to win much is to
win unfairly;—not quite yet, but he was near it. The wolfhood
was coming on him, unless some good fortune might save him.
There might, however, be such good fortune in store for him. As
Lady Elizabeth had said, a sheep that was very dark in colour
might become white again. If it be not so, what is all this
doctrine of repentance in which we believe?

Blackness in a male sheep in regard to the other sin is
venial blackness. Whether the teller of such a tale as this should
say so outright, may be matter of dispute; but, unless he say so,
the teller of this tale does not know how to tell his tale truly.
Blackness such as that will be all condoned, and the sheep
received into almost any flock, on condition, not of repentance
or humiliation or confession, but simply of change of practice.
The change of practice in certain circumstances and at a certain
period becomes expedient; and if it be made, as regards tints in
the wool of that nature, the sheep becomes as white as he is

SIR HARRY HOTSPUR OF HUMBLETHWAITE   45

needed to be. In this respect our sheep had been as black as any sheep, and at this present period of his life had need of much change before he would be fit for any decent social herding.

And then there are the shades of black which come from conviviality,—which we may call table blackness,—as to which there is an opinion constantly disseminated by the moral newspapers of the day, that there has come to be altogether an end of any such blackness among sheep who are gentlemen. To make up for this, indeed, there has been expressed by the piquant newspapers of the day an opinion that ladies are taking up the game which gentlemen no longer care to play. It may be doubted whether either expression has in it much of truth. We do not see ladies drunk, certainly, and we do not see gentlemen tumbling about as they used to do, because their fashion of drinking is not that of their grandfathers. But the love of wine has not gone out from among men; and men now are as prone as ever to indulge their loves. Our black sheep was very fond of wine,—and also of brandy, though he was wolf enough to hide his taste when occasion required it.

Very early in life he had come from France to live in England, and had been placed in a cavalry regiment, which had, unfortunately for him, been quartered either in London or its vicinity. And, perhaps equally unfortunate for him, he had in his own possession a small fortune of some £500 a year. This had not come to him from his father; and when his father had died in Paris, about two years before the date of our story, he had received no accession of regular income. Some couple of thousand of pounds had reached his hands from his father's effects, which had helped him through some of the immediately pressing difficulties of the day,—for his own income at that time had been altogether dissipated. And now he had received a much larger sum from his cousin, with an assurance, however, that the family property would not become his when he succeeded to the family title. He was so penniless at the time, so prone to live from hand to mouth, so little given to consideration of the future, that it may be doubted whether the sum given to him was not compensation in full for all that was to be withheld from him.

Still there was his chance with the heiress! In regarding this chance, he had very soon determined that he would marry his cousin if it might be within his power to do so. He knew, and fully appreciated, his own advantages. He was a handsome man,—tall for a Hotspur, but with the Hotspur fair hair and blue eyes, and well-cut features. There lacked, however, to him, that peculiar aspect of firmness about the temples which so strongly marked the countenance of Sir Harry and his daughter; and there had come upon him a *blasé* look, and certain outer signs of a bad life, which, however, did not mar his beauty, nor were they always apparent. The eye was not always bloodshot, nor was the hand constantly seen to shake. It may be said of him, both as to his moral and physical position, that he was on the edge of the precipice of degradation, but that there was yet a possibility of salvation.

He was living in a bachelor's set of rooms, at this time, in St. James's Street, for which, it must be presumed, that ready money was required. During the last winter he had horses in Northamptonshire, for the hire of which, it must be feared, that his prospects as heir to Humblethwaite had in some degree been pawned. At the present time he had a horse for Park riding, and he looked upon a good dinner, with good wine, as being due to him every day, as thoroughly as though he earned it. That he had never attempted to earn a shilling since the day on which he had ceased to be a soldier, now four years since, the reader will hardly require to be informed.

In spite of all his faults, this man enjoyed a certain social popularity for which many a rich man would have given a third of his income. Dukes and duchesses were fond of him; and certain persons, standing very high in the world, did not think certain parties were perfect without him. He knew how to talk enough, and yet not to talk too much. No one could say of him that he was witty, well-read, or given to much thinking; but he knew just what was wanted at this point of time or at that, and could give it. He could put himself forward, and could keep himself in the background. He could shoot well without wanting to shoot best. He could fetch and carry, but still do it always with an air of manly independence. He could subserve without an air of cringing. And then he looked like a gentleman.

Of all his well-to-do friends, perhaps he who really liked him best was the Earl of Altringham. George Hotspur was at this time something under thirty years of age, and the Earl was four years his senior. The Earl was a married man, with a family, a wife who also liked poor George, an enormous income, and a place in Scotland at which George always spent the three first weeks of grouse-shooting. The Earl was a kindly, good-humoured, liberal, but yet hard man of the world. He knew George Hotspur well, and would on no account lend him a shilling. He would not have given his friend money to extricate him from any difficulty. But he forgave the sinner all his sins, opened Castle Corry to him every year, provided him with the best of everything, and let him come and dine at Altringham House, in Carlton Gardens, as often almost as he chose during the London season. The Earl was very good to George, though he knew more about him than perhaps did any other man; but he would not bet with George, nor would he in any way allow George to make money out of him.

"Do you suppose that I want to win money of you?" he once said to our friend, in answer to a little proposition that was made to him at Newmarket. "I don't suppose you do," George had answered. "Then you may be sure that I don't want to lose any," the Earl had replied. And so the matter was ended, and George made no more propositions of the kind.

The two men were together at Tattersall's, looking at some horses which the Earl had sent up to be sold the day after the dinner in Bruton Street. "Sir Harry seems to be taking to you very kindly," said the Earl.

"Well,—yes; in a half-and-half sort of way."

"It isn't everybody that would give you £5,000, you know."

"I am not everybody's heir," said George.

"No; and you ain't his,—worse luck."

"I am,—in regard to the title."

"What good will that do you?"

"When he's gone, I shall be the head of the family. As far as I can understand these matters, he hasn't a right to leave the estates away from me."

"Power is right, my boy. Legal power is undoubtedly right."

"He should at any rate divide them. There are two distinct properties, and either of them would make me a rich man. I don't feel so very much obliged to him for his money,—though of course it was convenient."

"Very convenient, I should say, George. How do you get on with your cousin?"

"They watch me like a cat watches a mouse."

"Say a rat, rather, George. Don't you know they are right? Would not I do the same if she were my girl, knowing you as I do?"

"She might do worse, my Lord."

"I'll tell you what it is. He thinks that he might do worse. I don't doubt about that. All this matter of the family and the title, and the name, would make him ready to fling her to you,—if only you were a shade less dark a horse than you are."

"I don't know that I'm darker than others."

"Look here, old fellow; I don't often trouble you with advice, but I will now. If you'll set yourself steadily to work to live decently, if you'll tell Sir Harry the whole truth about your money matters, and really get into harness, I believe you may have her. Such a one as you never had such a chance before. But there's one thing you must do."

"What is the one thing?"

"Wash your hands altogether of Mrs. Morton. You'll have a difficulty, I know, and perhaps it will want more pluck than you've got. You haven't got pluck of that kind."

"You mean that I don't like to break a woman's heart?"

"Fiddlestick! Do you see that mare, there?"

"I was just looking at her. Why should you part with her?"

"She was the best animal in my stables, but she's given to eating the stable-boys; old Badger told me flat, that he wouldn't have her in the stables any longer. I pity the fellow who will buy her,—or rather his fellow. She killed a lad once in Brookborough's stables."

"Why don't you shoot her?"

"I can't afford to shoot horses, Captain Hotspur. I had my chance in buying her, and somebody else must have his chance now. That's the lot of them; one or two good ones, and the rest what I call rags. Do you think of what I've said; and be sure of this: Mrs. Morton and your cousin can't go on together. Ta, Ta!—I'm going across to my mother's."

George Hotspur, when he was left alone, did think a great deal about it. He was not a man prone to assure himself of a lady's favour without cause; and yet he did think that his cousin liked him. As to that terrible difficulty to which Lord Altringham had alluded, he knew that something must be done; but there were cruel embarrassments on that side of which even Altringham knew nothing. And then why should he do that which his friend had indicated to him, before he knew whether it would be necessary? As to taking Sir Harry altogether into his confidence about his money matters, that was clearly impossible. Heaven and earth! How could the one man speak such truths, or the other man listen to them? When money difficulties come of such nature as those which weighted the shoulders of poor George Hotspur, it is quite impossible that there should be any such confidence with any one. The sufferer cannot even make a confidant of himself, cannot even bring himself to look at his own troubles massed together. It was not the amount of his debts, but the nature of them, and the characters of the men with whom he had dealings, that were so terrible. Fifteen thousand pounds—less than one year's income from Sir Harry's property—would clear him of everything, as far as he could judge; but there could be no such clearing, otherwise than by money disbursed by himself, without a disclosure of dirt which he certainly would not dare to make to Sir Harry before his marriage.

But yet the prize to be won was so great, and there were so many reasons for thinking that it might possibly be within his grasp! If, after all, he might live to be Sir George Hotspur of Humblethwaite and Scarrowby! After thinking of it as well as he could, he determined that he would make the attempt; but as to those preliminaries to which Lord Altringham had referred, he would for the present leave them to chance.

Lord Altringham had been quite right when he told George Hotspur that he was deficient in a certain kind of pluck.

Chapter VI.

The Ball In Bruton Street.

Sir Harry vacillated, Lady Elizabeth doubted, and Cousin George was allowed to come to the ball. At this time, in the common understanding of such phrase, Emily Hotspur was heart-whole in regard to her cousin. Had she been made to know that he had gone away for ever,—been banished to some antipodes from which he never could return,—there would have been no lasting sorrow on her part, though there might have been some feeling which would have given her an ache for the moment. She had thought about him, as girls will think of men as to whom they own to themselves that it is possible that they may be in love with them some day;—and she liked him much. She also liked Lord Alfred, but the liking had been altogether of a different kind. In regard to Lord Alfred she had been quite sure, from the first days of her intercourse with him, that she could never be in love with him. He was to her no more than old Mr. Crutchley or young Mr. Latheby,—a man, and a good sort of man, but no more than a man. To worship Lord Alfred must be impossible to her. She had already conceived that it would be quite possible for her to worship her Cousin George in the teeth of all the hard things that she had heard of him. The reader may be sure that such a thought had passed through her mind when she asked her mother whether Cousin George was to be accepted as a black sheep or a white one?

The ball was a very grand affair, and Emily Hotspur was a very great lady. It had come to be understood that the successful suitor for her hand would be the future lord of Humblethwaite, and the power with which she was thus vested gave her a prestige and standing which can hardly be attained by mere wit and beauty, even when most perfectly combined. It was not that all who worshipped, either at a distance or with passing homage, knew the fact of the heiress-ship, or had ever heard of the £20,000 a year; but, given the status, and the worshippers will come. The word had gone forth in some mysterious way, and it was acknowledged that Emily Hotspur was a great young lady. Other young ladies, who were not great, allowed themselves to be postponed to her almost without jealousy, and young gentlemen without pretensions regarded her as one to whom they did not dare to ask to be introduced. Emily saw it all, and partly liked it, and partly despised it. But, even when despising it, she took advantage of it. The young gentlemen without pretensions were no more to her than the chairs and tables; and the young ladies who submitted to her and adored her,—were allowed to be submissive, and to adore. But of this she was quite sure,—that her Cousin George must some day be the head of her own family. He was a man whom she was bound to treat with attentive regard, if they who had the custody of her chose to place her in his company at all.

At this ball there were some very distinguished people indeed,—persons whom it would hardly be improper to call illustrious. There were two royal duchesses, one of whom was English, and no less than three princes. The Russian and French ambassadors were both there. There was the editor of the most influential newspaper of the day,—for a few minutes only; and the Prime Minister passed through the room in the course of the evening. Dukes and duchesses below the royal degree were common; and as for earls and countesses, and their daughters, they formed the ruck of the crowd. The Poet-laureate didn't come indeed, but was expected; and three Chinese mandarins of the first quality entered the room at eleven, and did not leave till one. Poor Lady Elizabeth suffered a great deal with those mandarins. From all this it will be seen that the ball was quite a success.

George Hotspur dined that day with Lord and Lady Altringham, and went with them to the ball in the evening. Lord Altringham, though his manner was airy and almost indifferent, was in truth most anxious that his friend should be put upon his feet by the marriage; and the Countess was so keen about it, that there was nothing in the way of innocent intrigue which she would not have done to accomplish it. She knew that George Hotspur was a rake, was a gambler, was in debt, was hampered by other difficulties, and all the rest of it; but she liked the man, and was therefore willing to believe that a rich marriage would put it all right. Emily Hotspur was nothing to her, nor was Sir Harry; but George had often made her own house pleasant to her, and therefore, to her thinking, deserved a wife with £20,000 a year. And then, if there might have been scruples under other circumstances, that fact of the baronetcy overcame them. It could not be wrong in one placed as was Lady Altringham to assist in preventing any separation of the title and the property. Of course George might probably squander all that he could squander; but that might be made right by settlements and entails. Lady Altringham was much more energetic than her husband, and had made out quite a plan of the manner in which George should proceed. She discussed the matter with him at great length. The one difficulty she was, indeed, obliged to slur over; but even that was not altogether omitted in her scheme. "Whatever incumbrances there may be, free yourself from them at once," she had advised.

"That is so very easy to say, Lady Altringham, but so difficult to do."

"As to debts, of course they can't be paid without money. Sir Harry will find it worth his while to settle any debts. But if there is anything else, stop it at once." Of course there was something else, and of course Lady Altringham knew what that something else was. She demanded, in accordance with her scheme, that George should lose no time. This was in May. It was known that Sir Harry intended to leave town early in June. "Of course you will take him at his word, and go to Humblethwaite when you leave us," she had said.

"No time has been named."

"Then you can name your own without difficulty. You will write from Castle Corry and say you are coming. That is, if it's not all settled by that time. Of course, it cannot be done in a minute, because Sir Harry must consent; but I should begin at once,—only, Captain Hotspur, leave nothing for them to find out afterwards. What is past they will forgive." Such had been Lady Altringham's advice, and no doubt she understood the matter which she had been discussing.

When George Hotspur entered the room, his cousin was dancing with a prince. He could see her as he stood speaking a few words to Lady Elizabeth. And in talking to Lady Elizabeth he did not talk as a stranger would, or a common guest. He had quite understood all that he might gain by assuming the intimacy of cousinhood, and he had assumed it. Lady Elizabeth was less weary than before when he stood by her, and accepted from his hand some little trifle of help, which was agreeable to her. And he showed himself in no hurry, and told her some little story that pleased her. What a pity it was that Cousin George should be a scamp, she thought, as he went on to greet Sir Harry.

And with Sir Harry he remained a minute or two. On such an occasion as this Sir Harry was all smiles, and quite willing to hear a little town gossip. "Come with the Altringhams, have you? I'm told Altringham has just sold all his horses. What's the meaning of that?"

"The old story, Sir Harry. He has weeded his stable, and got the buyers to think that they were getting the cream. There isn't a man in England knows better what he's about than Altringham."

Sir Harry smiled his sweetest, and answered with some good-humoured remark, but he said in his heart that "birds of a feather flock together," and that his cousin was—not a man of honour.

There are some things that no rogue can do. He can understand what it is to condemn roguery, to avoid it, to dislike it, to disbelieve in it;—but he cannot understand what it is to hate it. Cousin George had probably exaggerated the transaction of which he had spoken, but he had little thought that in doing so he had helped to imbue Sir Harry with a true idea of his own character.

George passed on, and saw his cousin, who was now standing up with a foreign ambassador. He just spoke to her as he passed her, calling her by her Christian name as he did so. She gave him her hand ever so graciously; and he, when he had gone on, returned and asked her to name a dance.

"But I don't think I've one left that I mean to dance," she said.

"Then give me one that you don't mean to dance," he answered. And of course she gave it to him.

It was an hour afterwards that he came to claim her promise, and she put her arm through his and stood up with him. There was no talk then of her not dancing, and she went whirling round the room with him in great bliss. Cousin George waltzed well. All such men do. It is a part of their stock-in-trade. On this evening Emily Hotspur thought that he waltzed better than any one else, and told him so. "Another turn? Of course I will with you, because you know what you're about."

"I'd blush if I'd time," said he.

"A great many gentlemen ought to blush, I know. That prince, whose name I always forget, and you, are the only men in the room who dance well, according to my ideas."

Then off they went again, and Emily was very happy. He could at least dance well, and there could be no reason why she should not enjoy his dancing well since he had been considered to be white enough to be asked to the ball.

But with George there was present at every turn and twist of the dance an idea that he was there for other work than that. He was tracking a head of game after which there would be many hunters. He had his advantages, and so would they have theirs. One of his was this,—that he had her there with him now, and he must use it. She would not fall into his mouth merely by being whirled round the room pleasantly. At last she was still, and consented to take a walk with him out of the room, somewhere out amidst the crowd, on the staircase if possible, so as to get a breath of fresh air. Of course he soon had her jammed into a corner out of which there was no immediate mode of escape.

"We shall never get away again," she said, laughing. Had she wanted to get away her tone and manner would have been very different.

"I wonder whether you feel yourself to be the same sort of person here that you are at Humblethwaite," he said.

"Exactly the same."

"To me you seem to be so different."

"In what way?"

"I don't think you are half so nice."

"How very unkind!"

Of course she was flattered. Of all flattery praise is the coarsest and least efficacious. When you would flatter a man, talk to him about himself, and criticise him, pulling him to pieces by comparison of some small present fault with his past conduct;—and the rule holds the same with a woman. To tell her that she looks well is feeble work; but complain to her woefully that there is something wanting at the present moment, something lacking from the usual high standard, some temporary loss of beauty, and your solicitude will prevail with her.

"And in what am I not nice? I am sure I'm trying to be as nice as I know how."

"Down at Humblethwaite you are simply yourself,—Emily Hotspur."

"And what am I here?"

"That formidable thing,—a success. Don't you feel yourself that you are lifted a little off your legs?"

"Not a bit;—not an inch. Why should I?"

"I fail to make you understand quite what I mean. Don't you feel that with all these princes and potentates you are forced to be something else than your natural self? Don't you know that you have to put on a special manner, and to talk in a special way? Does not the champagne fly to your head, more or less?"

"Of course, the princes and potentates are not the same as old Mrs. Crutchley, if you mean that."

"I am not blaming you, you know, only I cannot help being very anxious; and I found you so perfect at Humblethwaite that I cannot say that I like any change. You know I am to come to Humblethwaite again?"

"Of course you are."

"You go down next month, I believe?"

"Papa talks of going to Scarrowby for a few weeks. He always does every year, and it is so dull. Did you ever see Scarrowby?"

"Never."

"You ought to come there some day. You know one branch of the Hotspurs did live there for ever so long."

"Is it a good house?"

"Very bad indeed; but there are enormous woods, and the country is very wild, and everything is at sixes and sevens. However, of course you would not come, because it is in the middle of your London season. There would be ever so many things to keep you. You are a man who, I suppose, never was out of London in June in your life, unless some race meeting was going on."

"Do you really take me for such as that, Emily?"

"Yes, I do. That is what they tell me you are. Is it not true? Don't you go to races?"

"I should be quite willing to undertake never to put my foot on a racecourse again this minute. I will do so now if you will only ask it of me."

She paused a moment, half thinking that she would ask it, but at last she determined against it.

"No," she said; "if you think it proper to stay away, you can do so without my asking it. I have no right to make such a request. If you think races are bad, why don't you stay away of your own accord?"

"They are bad," he said.

"Then why do you go to them?"

"They are bad, and I do go to them. They are very bad, and I go to them very often. But I will stay away and never put my foot on another racecourse if you, my cousin, will ask me."

"That is nonsense."

"Try me. It shall not be nonsense. If you care enough about me to wish to save me from what is evil, you can do it. I care enough about you to give up the pursuit at your bidding."

As he said this he looked down into her eyes, and she knew that the full weight of his gaze was upon her. She knew that his words and his looks together were intended to impress her with some feeling of his love for her. She knew at the moment, too, that they gratified her. And she remembered also in the same moment that her Cousin George was a black sheep.

"If you cannot refrain from what is bad without my asking you," she said, "your refraining will do no good."

He was making her some answer, when she insisted on being taken away. "I must get into the dancing-room; I must indeed, George. I have already thrown over some poor wretch.

No, not yet, I see, however. I was not engaged for the quadrille; but I must go back and look after the people."

He led her back through the crowd; and as he did so he perceived that Sir Harry's eyes were fixed upon him. He did not much care for that. If he could carry his Cousin Emily, he thought that he might carry the Baronet also.

He could not get any special word with her again that night. He asked her for another dance, but she would not grant it to him. "You forget the princes and potentates to whom I have to attend," she said to him, quoting his own words.

He did not blame her, even to himself, judging by the importance which he attached to every word of private conversation which he could have with her, that she found it to be equally important. It was something gained that she should know that he was thinking of her. He could not be to her now like any cousin, or any other man, with whom she might dance three or four times without meaning anything. As he was aware of it, so must she be; and he was glad that she should feel that it was so.

"Emily tells me that you are going to Scarrowby next month," he said afterwards to Sir Harry.

Sir Harry frowned, and answered him very shortly, "Yes, we shall go there in June."

"Is it a large place?"

"Large? How do you mean? It is a good property."

"But the house?"

"The house is quite large enough for us," said Sir Harry; "but we do not have company there."

This was said in a very cold tone, and there was nothing more to be added. George, to do him justice, had not been fishing for an invitation to Scarrowby. He had simply been making conversation with the Baronet. It would not have suited him to go to Scarrowby, because by doing so he would have lost the power of renewing his visit to Humblethwaite. But Sir Harry in this interview had been so very ungracious,—and as George knew very well, because of the scene in the corner,—that there might be a doubt whether he would ever get to Humblethwaite at all. If he failed, however, it should not be for the want of audacity on his own part.

But, in truth, Sir Harry's blackness was still the result of vacillation. Though he would fain redeem this prodigal, if it were possible, and give him everything that was to be given; yet, when he saw the prodigal attempting to help himself to the good things, his wrath was aroused. George Hotspur, as he betook himself from Bruton Street to such other amusements as were at his command, meditated much over his position. He thought he could give up the racecourses; but he was sure that he could at any rate say that he would give them up.

Chapter VII.

Lady Altringham.

There was one more meeting between Cousin George and Emily Hotspur, before Sir Harry left London with his wife and daughter. On the Sunday afternoon following the ball he called in Bruton Street, and found Lord Alfred there. He knew that Lord Alfred had been refused, and felt it to be a matter of course that the suit would be pressed again. Nevertheless, he was quite free from animosity to Lord Alfred. He could see at a glance that there was no danger for him on that side. Lord Alfred was talking to Lady Elizabeth when he entered, and Emily was engaged with a bald-headed old gentleman with a little ribbon and a star. The bald-headed old gentleman soon departed, and then Cousin George, in some skillfully indirect way, took an opportunity of letting Emily know that he should not go to Goodwood this July.

"Not go to Goodwood?" said she, pretending to laugh. "It will be most unnatural, will it not? They'll hardly start the horses without you, I should think."

"They'll have to start them without me, at any rate." Of course she understood what he meant, and understood also why he had told her. But if his promise were true, so much good had been done,—and she sincerely believed that it was true. In what way could he make love to her better than by refraining from his evil ways for the sake of pleasing her? Other bald-headed old gentlemen and bewigged old ladies came in, and he had not time for another word. He bade her adieu, saying nothing now of his hope of meeting her in the autumn, and was very affectionate in his farewell to Lady Elizabeth. "I don't suppose I shall see Sir Harry before he starts. Say 'good-bye' for me."

"I will, George."

"I am so sorry you are going. It has been so jolly, coming in here of a Sunday, Lady Elizabeth, and you have been so good to me. I wish Scarrowby was at the bottom of the sea."

"Sir Harry wouldn't like that at all."

"I dare say not. And as such places must be, I suppose they ought to be looked after. Only why in June? Good-bye! We shall meet again some day." But not a word was said about Humblethwaite in September. He did not choose to mention the prospect of his autumn visit, and she did not dare to do so. Sir Harry had not renewed the offer, and she would not venture to do so in Sir Harry's absence.

June passed away,—as Junes do pass in London,—very gaily in appearance, very quickly in reality, with a huge outlay of money and an enormous amount of disappointment. Young ladies would not accept, and young men would not propose. Papas became cross and stingy, and mammas insinuated that daughters were misbehaving. The daughters fought their own battles, and became tired in the fighting of them, and many a one had declared to herself before July had come to an end that it was all vanity and vexation of spirit.

The Altringhams always went to Goodwood,—husband and wife. Goodwood and Ascot for Lady Altringham were festivals quite as sacred as were Epsom and Newmarket for the Earl. She looked forward to them all the year, learned all she could about the horses which were to run, was very anxious and energetic about her party, and, if all that was said was true, had

her little book. It was an institution also that George Hotspur
should be one of the party; and of all the arrangements usually
made, it was not the one which her Ladyship could dispense
with the easiest. George knew exactly what she liked to have
done, and how. The Earl himself would take no trouble, and
desired simply to be taken there and back and to find everything
that was wanted the very moment it was needed. And in all such
matters the Countess chose that the Earl should be indulged. But
it was necessary to have some one who would look after
something—who would direct the servants, and give the orders,
and be responsible. George Hotspur did it all admirably, and on
such occasions earned the hospitality which was given to him
throughout the year. At Goodwood he was almost indispensable
to Lady Altringham; but for this meeting she was willing to
dispense with him. "I tell you, Captain Hotspur, that you're not
to go," she said to him.

"Nonsense, Lady Altringham."

"What a child you are! Don't you know what depends on
it?"

"It does not depend on that."

"It may. Every little helps. Didn't you promise her that
you wouldn't?"

"She didn't take it in earnest."

"I tell you, you know nothing about a woman. She will
take it very much in earnest if you break your word."

"She'll never know."

"She will. She'll learn it. A girl like that learns
everything. Don't go; and let her know that you have not gone."

George Hotspur thought that he might go, and yet let her
know that he had not gone. An accomplished and successful lie
was to him a thing beautiful in itself,—an event that had come
off usefully, a piece of strategy that was evidence of skill, so
much gained on the world at the least possible outlay, an
investment from which had come profit without capital. Lady
Altringham was very hard on him, threatening him at one time

with the Earl's displeasure, and absolute refusal of his company. But he pleaded hard that his book would be ruinous to him if he did not go; that this was a pursuit of such a kind that a man could not give it up all of a moment; that he would take care that his name was omitted from the printed list of Lord Altringham's party; and that he ought to be allowed this last recreation. The Countess at last gave way, and George Hotspur did go to Goodwood.

With the success or failure of his book on that occasion our story is not concerned. He was still more flush of cash than usual, having something left of his cousin's generous present. At any rate, he came to no signal ruin at the races, and left London for Castle Corry on the 10th of August without any known diminution to his prospects. At that time the Hotspurs were at Humblethwaite with a party; but it had been already decided that George should not prepare to make his visit till September. He was to write from Castle Corry. All that had been arranged between him and the Countess, and from Castle Corry he did write:—

> DEAR LADY ELIZABETH,—
>
> Sir Harry was kind enough to say last winter that I might come to Humblethwaite again this autumn. Will you be able to take me in on the 2nd September? we have about finished with Altringham's house, and Lady A. has had enough of me. They remain here till the end of this month. With kind regards to Sir Harry and Emily,
>
> Believe me, yours always,
>
> GEORGE HOTSPUR.

Nothing could be simpler than this note, and yet every word of it had been weighed and dictated by Lady Altringham. "That won't do at all. You mustn't seem to be so eager," she had said, when he showed her the letter as prepared by himself. "Just write as you would do if you were coming here." Then she sat down, and made the copy for him.

There was very great doubt and there was much deliberation over that note at Humblethwaite. The invitation had doubtless been given, and Sir Harry did not wish to turn against his own flesh and blood,—to deny admittance to his house to the man who was the heir to his title. Were he to do so, he must give some reason; he must declare some quarrel; he must say boldly that all intercourse between them was to be at an end; and he must inform Cousin George that this strong step was taken because Cousin George was a—blackguard! There was no other way of escape left. And then Cousin George had done nothing since the days of the London intimacies to warrant such treatment; he had at least done nothing to warrant such treatment at the hands of Sir Harry. And yet Sir Harry thoroughly wished that his cousin was at Jerusalem. He still vacillated, but his vacillation did not bring him nearer to his cousin's side of the case. Every little thing that he saw and heard made him know that his cousin was a man to whom he could not give his daughter even for the sake of the family, without abandoning his duty to his child. At this moment, while he was considering George's letter, it was quite clear to him that George should not be his son-in-law; and yet the fact that the property and the title might be brought together was not absent from his mind when he gave his final assent. "I don't suppose she cares for him," he said to his wife.

"She's not in love with him, if you mean that."

"What else should I mean?" he said, crossly.

"She may learn to be in love with him."

"She had better not. She must be told. He may come for a week. I won't have him here for longer. Write to him and say that we shall be happy to have him from the second to the ninth. Emily must be told that I disapprove of him, but that I can't avoid opening my house to him."

These were the most severe words he had ever spoken about Cousin George, but then the occasion had become very critical. Lady Elizabeth's reply was as follows:—

My Dear Cousin George,—

Sir Harry and I will be very happy to have you on the second, as you propose, and hope you will stay till the eleventh.

Yours sincerely,

Elizabeth Hotspur.

He was to come on a Saturday, but she did not like to tell him to go on a Saturday, because of the following day. Where could the poor fellow be on the Sunday? She therefore stretched her invitation for two days beyond the period sanctioned by Sir Harry.

"It's not very gracious," said George, as he showed the note to Lady Altringham.

"I don't like it the less on that account. It shows that they're afraid about her, and they wouldn't be afraid without cause."

"There is not much of that, I fancy."

"They oughtn't to have a chance against you,—not if you play your game well. Even in ordinary cases the fathers and mothers are beaten by the lovers nine times out of ten. It is only when the men are oafs and louts that they are driven off. But with you, with your cousinship, and half-heirship, and all your practice, and the family likeness, and the rest of it, if you only take a little trouble—"

"I'll take any amount of trouble."

"No, you won't. You'll deny yourself nothing, and go through no ordeal that is disagreeable to you. I don't suppose your things are a bit better arranged in London than they were in the spring." She looked at him as though waiting for an answer, but he was silent. "It's too late for anything of that kind now, but still you may do very much. Make up your mind to this, that you'll ask Miss Hotspur to be your wife before you leave— what's the name of the place?"

"I have quite made up my mind to that, Lady Altringham."

"As to the manner of doing it, I don't suppose that I can teach you anything."

"I don't know about that."

"At any rate I shan't try. Only remember this. Get her to promise to be firm, and then go at once to Sir Harry. Don't let there be an appearance of doubt in speaking to him. And if he tells you of the property,—angrily I mean,—then do you tell him of the title. Make him understand that you give as much as you get. I don't suppose he will yield at first. Why should he? You are not the very best young man about town, you know. But if you get her, he must follow. She looks like one that would stick to it, if she once had said it."

Thus prompted George Hotspur went from Castle Corry to Humblethwaite. I wonder whether he was aware of the extent of the friendship of his friend, and whether he ever considered why it was that such a woman should be so anxious to assist him in making his fortune, let it be at what cost it might to others! Lady Altringham was not the least in love with Captain Hotspur, was bound to him by no tie whatsoever, would suffer no loss in the world should Cousin George come to utter and incurable ruin; but she was a woman of energy, and, as she liked the man, she was zealous in his friendship.

Chapter VIII.

Airey Force.

Lady Elizabeth had been instructed by Sir Harry to warn her daughter not to fall in love with Cousin George during his visit to Humblethwaite; and Lady Elizabeth was, as a wife, accustomed to obey her husband in all things. But obedience in this matter was very difficult. Such a caution as that received is not easily given even between a mother and a child, and is especially difficult when the mother is unconsciously aware of her child's superiority to herself. Emily was in all respects the bigger woman of the two, and was sure to get the best of it in any such cautioning. It is so hard to have to bid a girl, and a good girl too, not to fall in love with a particular man! There is left among us at any rate so much of reserve and assumed delicacy as to require us to consider, or pretend to consider on the girl's behalf, that of course she won't fall in love. We know that she will, sooner or later; and probably as much sooner as opportunity may offer. That is our experience of the genus girl in the general; and we quite approve of her for her readiness to do so. It is, indeed, her nature; and the propensity has been planted in her for wise purposes. But as to this or that special sample of the genus girl, in reference to this or that special sample of the genus young man, we always feel ourselves bound to take it as a matter of course that there can be nothing of the kind, till the thing is done. Any caution on the matter is therefore difficult and disagreeable, as conveying almost an insult. Mothers in well-regulated families do not caution their daughters in reference to special young men. But Lady Elizabeth had been desired by her husband to give the caution, and must in some sort obey the instruction. Two days before George's arrival she endeavoured to do as she was told; not with the most signal success.

"Your Cousin George is coming on Saturday."

"So I heard Papa say."

"Your Papa gave him a sort of invitation when he was here last time, and so he has proposed himself."

"Why should not he? It seems very natural. He is the nearest relation we have got, and we all like him."

"I don't think your Papa does like him."

"I do."

"What I mean is your Papa doesn't approve of him. He goes to races, and bets, and all that kind of thing. And then your Papa thinks that he's over head and ears in debt."

"I don't know anything about his debts. As for his going to races, I believe he has given them up. I am sure he would if he were asked." Then there was a pause, for Lady Elizabeth hardly knew how to pronounce her caution. "Why shouldn't Papa pay his debts?"

"My dear!"

"Well, Mamma, why shouldn't he? And why shouldn't Papa let him have the property; I mean, leave it to him instead of to me?"

"If your brother had lived—"

"He didn't live, Mamma. That has been our great misfortune. But so it is; and why shouldn't George be allowed to take his place? I'm sure it would be for the best. Papa thinks so much about the name, and the family, and all that."

"My dear, you must leave him to do as he thinks fit in all such matters. You may be sure that he will do what he believes to be his duty. What I was going to say was this—" And, instead of saying it, Lady Elizabeth still hesitated.

"I know what you want to say, Mamma, just as well as though the words were out of your mouth. You want to make me to understand that George is a black sheep."

"I'm afraid he is."

"But black sheep are not like blackamoors; they may be washed white. You said so yourself the other day."

"Did I, my dear?"

"Certainly you did; and certainly they may. Why, Mamma, what is all religion but the washing of black sheep white; making the black a little less black, scraping a spot white here and there?"

"I am afraid your Cousin George is beyond washing."

"Then Mamma, all I can say is, he oughtn't to come here. Mind, I think you wrong him. I daresay he has been giddy and fond of pleasure; but if he is so bad as you say, Papa should tell him at once not to come. As far as I am concerned, I don't believe he is so bad; and I shall be glad to see him."

There was no cautioning a young woman who could reason in this way, and who could look at her mother as Emily looked. It was not, at least, within the power of Lady Elizabeth to do so. And yet she could not tell Sir Harry of her failure. She thought that she had expressed the caution; and she thought also that her daughter would be wise enough to be guided,—not by her mother's wisdom, but by the words of her father. Poor dear woman! She was thinking of it every hour of the day; but she said nothing more on the subject, either to her daughter or to Sir Harry.

The black sheep came, and made one of a number of numerous visitors. It had been felt that the danger would be less among a multitude; and there was present a very excellent young man, as to whom there were hopes. Steps had not been taken about this excellent young man as had been done in reference to Lord Alfred; but still there were hopes. He was the eldest son of a Lincolnshire squire, a man of fair property and undoubted family; but who, it was thought, would not object to merge the name of Thoresby in that of Hotspur. Nothing came of the young man, who was bashful, and to whom Miss Hotspur certainly gave no entertainment of a nature to remove his bashfulness. But when the day for George's coming had been fixed, Sir Harry thought it expedient to write to young Thoresby and accelerate a visit which had been previously proposed. Sir Harry as he did so almost hated himself for his anxiety to dispose of his daughter. He was a gentleman, every inch of him; and he thoroughly desired to do his duty. He knew, however, that there was much in his feelings of which he could not but be ashamed. And yet, if something were not done to assist his girl in a right disposal of all that she had to bestow with her hand, how was it probable that it could be disposed aright?

The black sheep came, and found young Thoresby and some dozen other strangers in the house. He smiled upon them all, and before the first evening was over had made himself the popular man of the house. Sir Harry, like a fool as he was, had given his cousin only two fingers, and had looked black at their first meeting. Nothing could be gained by conduct such as that with such a guest. Before the gentlemen left the dinner-table on the first day even he had smiled and joked and had asked questions about "Altringham's mountains." "The worst of you fellows who go to Scotland is that you care nothing for real sport when you come down south afterwards." All this conversation about Lord Altringham's grouse and the Scotch mountains helped George Hotspur, so that when he went into the drawing-room he was in the ascendant. Many men have learned the value of such ascendancy, and most men have known the want of it.

Poor Lady Elizabeth had not a chance with Cousin George. She succumbed to him at once, not knowing why, but feeling that she herself became bright, amusing, and happy when talking to him. She was a woman not given to familiarities; but she did become familiar with him, allowing him little liberties of expression which no other man would take with her, and putting them all down to the score of cousinhood. He might be a black sheep. She feared there could be but little doubt that he was one. But, from her worsted-work up to the demerits of her dearest friend, he did know how to talk better than any other young man she knew. To Emily, on that first evening, he said very little. When he first met her he had pressed her hand, and looked into her eyes, and smiled on her with a smile so sweet that it was as though a god had smiled on her. She had made up her mind that he should be nothing to her,—nothing beyond a dear cousin; nevertheless, her eye had watched him during the whole hour of dinner, and, not knowing that it was so, she had waited for his coming to them in the evening. Heavens and earth! what an oaf was that young Thoresby as the two stood together near the door! She did not want her cousin to come and talk to her, but she listened and laughed within herself as she saw how pleased was her mother by the attentions of the black sheep.

One word Cousin George did say to Emily Hotspur that night, just as the ladies were leaving the room. It was said in a whisper, with a little laugh, with that air of half joke half earnest which may be so efficacious in conversation: "I did not go to Goodwood, after all."

She raised her eyes to his for a quarter of a second, thanking him for his goodness in refraining. "I don't believe that he is really a black sheep at all," she said to herself that night, as she laid her head upon her pillow.

After all, the devil fights under great disadvantages, and has to carry weights in all his races which are almost unfair. He lies as a matter of course, believing thoroughly in lies, thinking that it is by lies chiefly that he must make his running good; and yet every lie he tells, after it has been told and used, remains as an additional weight to be carried. When you have used your lie gracefully and successfully, it is hard to bury it and get it well out of sight. It crops up here and there against you, requiring more lies; and at last, too often, has to be admitted as a lie, most usually so admitted in silence, but still admitted,—to be forgiven or not, according to the circumstances of the case. The most perfect forgiveness is that which is extended to him who is known to lie in everything. The man has to be taken, lies and all, as a man is taken with a squint, or a harelip, or a bad temper. He has an uphill game to fight, but when once well known, he does not fall into the difficulty of being believed.

George Hotspur's lie was believed. To our readers it may appear to have been most gratuitous, unnecessary, and inexpedient. The girl would not have quarrelled with him for going to the races,—would never have asked anything about it. But George knew that he must make his running. It would not suffice that she should not quarrel with him. He had to win her, and it came so natural to him to lie! And the lie was efficacious; she was glad to know that he stayed away from the races—for her sake. Had it not been for her sake? She would not bid him stay away, but she was so glad that he had stayed! The lie was very useful;—if it only could have been buried and put out of sight when used!

There was partridge-shooting for four days; not good shooting, but work which carried the men far from home, and enabled Sir Harry to look after his cousin. George, so looked after, did not dare to say that on any day he would shirk the shooting. But Sir Harry, as he watched his cousin, gradually lost his keenness for watching him. Might it not be best that he should let matters arrange themselves? This young squire from Lincolnshire was evidently an oaf. Sir Harry could not even cherish a hope on that side. His girl was very good, and she had been told, and the work of watching went so much against the grain with him! And then, added to it all, was the remembrance that if the worst came to the worst, the title and property would be kept together. George Hotspur might have fought his fight, we think, without the aid of his lie.

On the Friday the party was to some extent broken up. The oaf and sundry other persons went away. Sir Harry had thought that the cousin would go on the Saturday, and had been angry with his wife because his orders on that head had not been implicitly obeyed. But when the Friday came, and George offered to go in with him to Penrith, to hear some case of fish-poaching which was to be brought before the magistrates, he had forgiven the offence. George had a great deal to say about fish, and then went on to say a good deal about himself. If he could only get some employment, a farm, say, where he might have hunting, how good it would be! For he did not pretend to any virtuous abnegation of the pleasures of the world, but was willing,—so he said,—to add to them some little attempt to earn his own bread. On this day Sir Harry liked his cousin better than he had ever done before, though he did not even then place the least confidence in his cousin's sincerity as to the farm and the earning of bread.

On their return to the Hall on Friday they found that a party had been made to go to Ulleswater on the Saturday. A certain Mrs. Fitzpatrick was staying in the house, who had never seen the lake, and the carriage was to take them to Airey Force. Airey Force, as everybody knows, is a waterfall near to the shores of the lake, and is the great lion of the Lake scenery on that side of the mountains. The waterfall was full fifteen miles from Humblethwaite, but the distance had been done before, and could be done again. Emily, Mrs. Fitzpatrick, and two other young ladies were to go. Mr. Fitzpatrick would sit on the box. There was a youth there also who had left school and not yet gone to college. He was to be allowed to drive a dog-cart. Of course George Hotspur was ready to go in the dog-cart with him. George had determined from the commencement of his visit, when he began to foresee that this Saturday would be more at his command than any other day, that on this Saturday he would make or mar his fortune for life. He had perceived that his cousin was cautious with him, that he would be allowed but little scope for love-making, that she was in some sort afraid of him; but he perceived also that in a quiet undemonstrative way she was very gracious to him. She never ignored him, as young ladies will sometimes ignore young men, but thought of him even in his absence, and was solicitous for his comfort. He was clever enough to read little signs, and was sure at any rate that she liked him.

"Why did you not postpone the party till George was gone?" Sir Harry said to his wife.

"The Fitzpatricks also go on Monday," she answered, "and we could not refuse them."

Then again it occurred to Sir Harry that life would not be worth having if he was to be afraid to allow his daughter to go to a picnic in company with her cousin.

There is a bridge across the water at the top of Airey Force, which is perhaps one of the prettiest spots in the whole of our Lake country. The entire party on their arrival of course went up to the bridge, and then the entire party of course descended. How it happened that in the course of the afternoon George and Emily were there again, and were there unattended, who can tell? If she had meant to be cautious, she must very much have changed her plans in allowing herself to be led thither. And as he stood there, with no eye resting on them, his arm was round her waist and she was pressed to his side.

"Dearest, dearest," he said, "may I believe that you love me?"

"I have said so. You may believe it if you will."

She did not attempt to make the distance greater between them. She leant against him willingly.

"Dear George, I do love you. My choice has been made. I have to trust to you for everything."

"You shall never trust in vain," he said.

"You must reform, you know," she said, turning round and looking up into his face with a smile. "They say that you have been wild. You must not be wild any more, sir."

"I will reform. I have reformed. I say it boldly; I have become an altered man since I knew you. I have lived with one hope, and even the hope alone has changed me. Now I have got all that I have hoped for. Oh, Emily, I wish you knew how much I love you!"

They were there on the bridge, or roaming together alone among the woods, for nearly an hour after that, till Mrs. Fitzpatrick, who knew the value of the prize and the nature of the man, began to fear that she had been remiss in her duty as chaperon. As Emily came down and joined the party at last, she was perfectly regardless either of their frowns or smiles. There had been one last compact made between the lovers.

"George," she had said, "whatever it may cost us, let there be no secrets."

"Of course not," he replied.

"I will tell Mamma to-night; and you must tell Papa. You will promise me?"

"Certainly. It is what I should insist on doing myself. I could not stay in his house under other circumstances. But you too must promise me one thing, Emily."

"What is it?"

"You will be true to me, even though he should refuse his consent?"

She paused before she answered him.

"I will be true to you. I cannot be otherwise than true to you. My love was a thing to give, but when given I cannot take it back. I will be true to you, but of course we cannot be married unless Papa consents."

He urged her no further. He was too wise to think it possible that he could do so without injuring his cause. Then they found the others, and Emily made her apologies to Mrs. Fitzpatrick for the delay with a quiet dignity that struck her Cousin George almost with awe. How had it been that such a one as he had won so great a creature?

George, as he was driven home by his young companion, was full of joyous chatter and light small talk. He had done a good stroke of business, and was happy. If only the Baronet could be brought round, all the troubles which had enveloped him since a beard had first begun to grow on his chin would disappear as a mist beneath the full rays of the sun; or even if there still might be a trouble or two,—and as he thought of his prospects he remembered that they could not all be made to disappear in the mist fashion,—there would be that which would gild the clouds. At any rate he had done a good stroke of business. And he loved the girl too. He thought that of all the girls he had seen about town, or about the country either, she was the bonniest and the brightest and the most clever. It might well have been that a poor devil like he in search of an heiress might have been forced to put up with personal disadvantages,— with age, with plain looks, with vulgar manners, with low birth; but here, so excellent was his fortune, there was everything which fortune could give! Love her? Of course he loved her. He would do anything on earth for her. And how jolly they would be together when they got hold of their share of that £20,000 a year! And how jolly it would be to owe nothing to anybody! As he thought of this, however, there came upon him the reminiscence of a certain Captain Stubber, and the further reminiscence of a certain Mr. Abraham Hart, with both of whom he had dealings; and he told himself that it would behove him to call up all his pluck when discussing those gentlemen and their dealings, with the Baronet. He was sure that the Baronet would not like Captain Stubber nor Mr. Hart, and that a good deal of pluck would be needed. But on the whole he had done a great stroke of business; and, as a consequence of his success, talked and chatted all the way home, till the youth who was driving him thought that George was about the nicest fellow that he had ever met.

Emily Hotspur, as she took her place in the carriage, was very silent. She also had much of which to think, much on

which—as she dreamed—to congratulate herself. But she could
not think of it and talk at the same time. She had made her little
apology with graceful ease. She had just smiled,—but the smile
was almost a rebuke,—when one of her companions had
ventured on the beginning of some little joke as to her company,
and then she had led the way to the carriage. Mrs. Fitzpatrick
and the two girls were nothing to her now, let them suspect what
they choose or say what they might. She had given herself away,
and she triumphed in the surrender. The spot on which he had
told her of his love should be sacred to her for ever. It was a joy
to her that it was near to her own home, the home that she would
give to him, so that she might go there with him again and again.
She had very much to consider and to remember. A black sheep!
No! Of all the flock he should be the least black. It might be that
in the energy of his pleasures he had exceeded other men, as he
did exceed all other men in everything that he did and said. Who
was so clever? who so bright? who so handsome, so full of
poetry and of manly grace? How sweet was his voice, how fine
his gait, how gracious his smile! And then in his brow there was
that look of command which she had ever recognized in her
father's face as belonging to his race as a Hotspur,—only added
to it was a godlike beauty which her father never could have
possessed.

　　　　She did not conceal from herself that there might be
trouble with her father. And yet she was not sure but that upon
the whole he would be pleased after a while. Humblethwaite and
the family honours would still go together, if he would sanction
this marriage; and she knew how he longed in his heart that it
might be so. For a time probably he might be averse to her
prayers. Should it be so, she would simply give him her word
that she would never during his lifetime marry without his
permission,—and then she would be true to her troth. As to her
truth in that respect there could be no doubt. She had given her
word; and that, for a Hotspur, must be enough.

She could not talk as she thought of all this, and therefore had hardly spoken when George appeared at the carriage door to give the ladies a hand as they came into the house. To her he was able to give one gentle pressure as she passed on; but she did not speak to him, nor was it necessary that she should do so. Had not everything been said already?

Chapter IX.

"I Know What You Are."

The scene which took place that night between the mother and daughter may be easily conceived. Emily told her tale, and told it in a manner which left no doubt of her persistency. She certainly meant it. Lady Elizabeth had almost expected it. There are evils which may come or may not; but as to which, though we tell ourselves that they may still be avoided, we are inwardly almost sure that they will come. Such an evil in the mind of Lady Elizabeth had been Cousin George. Not but what she herself would have liked him for a son-in-law had it not been so certain that he was a black sheep.

"Your father will never consent to it, my dear."

"Of course, Mamma, I shall do nothing unless he does."

"You will have to give him up."

"No, Mamma, not that; that is beyond what Papa can demand of me. I shall not give him up, but I certainly shall not marry him without Papa's consent, or yours."

"Nor see him?"

"Well; if he does not come I cannot see him."

"Nor correspond with him?"

"Certainly not, if Papa forbids it."

After that, Lady Elizabeth did give way to a considerable extent. She did not tell her daughter that she considered it at all probable that Sir Harry would yield; but she made it to be understood that she herself would do so if Sir Harry would be persuaded. And she acknowledged that the amount of obedience promised by Emily was all that could be expected. "But, Mamma," said Emily, before she left her mother, "do you not know that you love him yourself?"

"Love is such a strong word, my dear."

"It is not half strong enough," said Emily, pressing her two hands together. "But you do, Mamma?"

"I think he is very agreeable, certainly."

"And handsome?—only that goes for nothing."

"Yes, he is a fine-looking man."

"And clever? I don't know how it is; let there be who there may in the room, he is always the best talker."

"He knows how to talk, certainly."

"And, Mamma, don't you think that there is a something,—I don't know what,—something not at all like other men about him that compels one to love him? Oh, Mamma, do say something nice to me! To me he is everything that a man should be."

"I wish he were, my dear."

"As for the sort of life he has been leading, spending more money than he ought, and all that kind of thing, he has promised to reform it altogether; and he is doing it now. At any rate, you must admit, Mamma, that he is not false."

"I hope not, my dear."

"Why do you speak in that way, Mamma? Does he talk like a man that is false? Have you ever known him to be false? Don't be prejudiced, Mamma, at any rate."

The reader will understand that when the daughter had brought her mother as far as this, the elder lady was compelled to say "something nice" at last. At any rate there was a loving embrace between them, and an understanding that the mother would not exaggerate the difficulties of the position either by speech or word.

"Of course you will have to see your papa to-morrow morning," Lady Elizabeth said.

"George will tell him everything to-night," said Emily. She as she went to her bed did not doubt but what the difficulties would melt. Luckily for her,—so luckily!—it happened that her lover possessed by his very birth a right which, beyond all other possessions, would recommend him to her father. And then had not the man himself all natural good gifts to recommend him? Of course he had not money or property, but she had, or would have, property; and of all men alive her father was the least disposed to be greedy. As she half thought of it and half dreamt of it in her last waking moments of that important day, she was almost altogether happy. It was so sweet to know that she possessed the love of him whom she loved better than all the world beside.

Cousin George did not have quite so good a time of it that night. The first thing he did on his return from Ulleswater to Humblethwaite was to write a line to his friend Lady Altringham. This had been promised, and he did so before he had seen Sir Harry.

> DEAR LADY A.—
>
> I have been successful with my younger cousin. She is the bonniest, and the best, and the brightest girl that ever lived, and I am the happiest fellow. But I have not as yet seen the Baronet. I am to do so to-night, and will report progress to-morrow. I doubt I shan't find him so bonny and so good and so bright. But, as you say, the young birds ought to be too strong for the old ones.
>
> —Yours most sincerely,
>
> G. H.

This was written while he was dressing, and was put into the letter-box by himself as he came downstairs. It was presumed that the party had dined at the Falls; but there was "a tea" prepared for them on an extensive scale. Sir Harry, suspecting nothing, was happy and almost jovial with Mr. Fitzpatrick and the two young ladies. Emily said hardly a word. Lady Elizabeth, who had not as yet been told, but already suspected something, was very anxious. George was voluble, witty, and perhaps a little too loud. But as the lad who was going to Oxford, and who had drank a good deal of champagne and was now drinking sherry, was loud also, George's manner was not specially observed. It was past ten before they got up from the table, and nearly eleven before George was able to whisper a word to the Baronet. He almost shirked it for that night, and would have done so had he not remembered how necessary it was that Emily should know that his pluck was good. Of course she would be asked to abandon him. Of course she would be told that it was her duty to give him up. Of course she would give him up unless he could get such a hold upon her heart as to make her doing so impossible to her. She would have to learn that he was an unprincipled spendthrift,—nay worse than that, as he hardly scrupled to tell himself. But he need not weight his own character with the further burden of cowardice. The Baronet could not eat him, and he would not be afraid of the Baronet. "Sir Harry," he whispered, "could you give me a minute or two before we go to bed?" Sir Harry started as though he had been stung, and looked his cousin sharply in the face without answering him. George kept his countenance, and smiled.

"I won't keep you long," he said.

"You had better come to my room," said Sir Harry, gruffly, and led the way into his own sanctum. When there, he sat down in his accustomed arm-chair without offering George a seat, but George soon found a seat for himself. "And now what is it?" said Sir Harry, with his blackest frown.

"I have asked my cousin to be my wife."

"What! Emily?"

"Yes, Emily; and she has consented. I now ask for your approval." We must give Cousin George his due, and acknowledge that he made his little request exactly as he would have done had he been master of ten thousand a year of his own, quite unencumbered.

"What right had you, sir, to speak to her without coming to me first?"

"One always does, I think, go to the girl first," said George.

"You have disgraced yourself, sir, and outraged my hospitality. You are no gentleman!"

"Sir Harry, that is strong language."

"Strong! Of course it is strong. I mean it to be strong. I shall make it stronger yet if you attempt to say another word to her."

"Look here, Sir Harry, I am bound to bear a good deal from you, but I have a right to explain."

"You have a right, sir, to go away from this, and go away you shall."

"Sir Harry, you have told me that I am not a gentleman."

"You have abused my kindness to you. What right have you, who have not a shilling in the world, to speak to my daughter? I won't have it, and let that be an end of it. I won't have it. And I must desire that you will leave Humblethwaite to-morrow. I won't have it."

"It is quite true that I have not a shilling."

"Then what business have you to speak to my daughter?"

"Because I have that which is worth many shillings, and which you value above all your property. I am the heir to your name and title. When you are gone, I must be the head of this family. I do not in the least quarrel with you for choosing to leave your property to your own child, but I have done the best I could to keep the property and the title together. I love my cousin."

"I don't believe in your love, sir."

"If that is all, I do not doubt but that I can satisfy you."

"It is not all; and it is not half all. And it isn't because you are a pauper. You know it all as well as I do, without my telling you, but you drive me to tell you."

"Know what, sir?"

"Though you hadn't a shilling, you should have had her if you could win her,—had your life been even fairly decent. The title must go to you,—worse luck for the family. You can talk well enough, and what you say is true. I would wish that they should go together."

"Of course it will be better."

"But, sir,—" then Sir Henry paused.

"Well, Sir Harry?"

"You oblige me to speak out. You are such a one, that I do not dare to let you have my child. Your life is so bad, that I should not be justified in doing so for any family purpose. You would break her heart."

"You wrong me there, altogether."

"You are a gambler."

"I have been, Sir Harry."

"And a spendthrift?"

"Well—yes; as long as I had little or nothing to spend."

"I believe you are over head and ears in debt now, in spite of the assistance you have had from me within twelve months."

Cousin George remembered the advice which had been given him, that he should conceal nothing from his cousin. "I do owe some money certainly," he said.

"And how do you mean to pay it?"

"Well—if I marry Emily, I suppose that—you will pay it."

"That's cool, at any rate."

"What can I say, Sir Harry?"

"I would pay it all, though it were to half the property—"

"Less than a year's income would clear off every shilling I owe, Sir Harry."

"Listen to me, sir. Though it were ten years' income, I would pay it all, if I thought that the rest would be kept with the title, and that my girl would be happy."

"I will make her happy."

"But, sir, it is not only that you are a gambler and spendthrift, and an unprincipled debtor without even a thought of paying. You are worse than this. There;—I am not going to call you names. I know what you are, and you shall not have my daughter."

George Hotspur found himself compelled to think for a few moments before he could answer a charge so vague, and yet, as he knew, so well founded. Nevertheless he felt that he was progressing. His debts would not stand in his way, if only he could make this rich father believe that in other matters his daughter would not be endangered by the marriage. "I don't quite know what you mean, Sir Harry. I am not going to defend myself. I have done much of which I am ashamed. I was turned very young upon the world, and got to live with rich people when I was myself poor. I ought to have withstood the temptation, but I didn't, and I got into bad hands. I don't deny it. There is a horrid Jew has bills of mine now."

"What have you done with that five thousand pounds?"

"He had half of it; and I had to settle for the last Leger, which went against me."

"It is all gone?"

"Pretty nearly. I don't pretend but what I have been very reckless as to money; I am ready to tell you the truth about everything. I don't say that I deserve her; but I do say this,—that I should not have thought of winning her, in my position, had it not been for the title. Having that in my favour I do not think that I was misbehaving to you in proposing to her. If you will trust me now, I will be as grateful and obedient a son as any man ever had."

He had pleaded his cause well, and he knew it. Sir Harry also felt that his cousin had made a better case than he would have believed to be possible. He was quite sure that the man was a scamp, utterly untrustworthy, and yet the man's pleading for himself had been efficacious. He sat silent for full five minutes before he spoke again, and then he gave judgment as follows: "You will go away without seeing her to-morrow."

"If you wish it."

"And you will not write to her."

"Only a line."

"Not a word," said Sir Harry, imperiously.

"Only a line, which I will give open to you. You can do with it as you please."

"And as you have forced upon me the necessity, I shall make inquiries in London as to your past life. I have heard things which perhaps may be untrue."

"What things, Sir Harry?"

"I shall not demean myself or injure you by repeating them, unless I find cause to believe they are true. I do believe that the result will be such as to make me feel that in justice to my girl I cannot allow you to become her husband. I tell you so fairly. Should the debts you owe be simple debts, not dishonourably contracted, I will pay them."

"And then she shall be mine?"

"I will make no such promise. You had better go now. You can have the carriage to Penrith as early as you please in the morning; or to Carlisle if you choose to go north. I will make your excuses to Lady Elizabeth. Good night."

Cousin George stood for a second in doubt, and then shook hands with the Baronet. He reached Penrith the next morning soon after ten, and breakfasted alone at the hotel.

There were but very few words spoken on the occasion between the father and daughter, but Emily did succeed in learning pretty nearly the truth of what had taken place. On the Monday her mother gave her the following note:—

DEAREST,—

At your father's bidding, I have gone suddenly. You will understand why I have done so. I shall try to do just as he would have me; but you will, I know, be quite sure that I should never give you up.

—Yours for ever and ever,

G. H.

The father had thought much of it, and at last had determined that Emily should have the letter.

In the course of the week there came other guests to Humblethwaite, and it so chanced that there was a lady who knew the Altringhams, who had unfortunately met the Altringhams at Goodwood, and who, most unfortunately, stated in Emily's hearing that she had seen George Hotspur at Goodwood.

"He was not there," said Emily, quite boldly.

"Oh, yes; with the Altringhams, as usual. He is always with them at Goodwood."

"He was not at the last meeting," said Emily, smiling.

The lady said nothing till her lord was present, and then appealed to him. "Frank, didn't you see George Hotspur with the Altringhams at Goodwood, last July?"

"To be sure I did, and lost a pony to him on Eros."

The lady looked at Emily, who said nothing further; but she was still quite convinced that George Hotspur had not been at those Goodwood races.

It is so hard, when you have used a lie commodiously, to bury it, and get well rid of it.

Chapter X.

Mr. Hart And Captain Stubber.

When George Hotspur left Humblethwaite, turned out of the house by the angry Baronet early in the morning,—as the reader will remember,—he was at his own desire driven to Penrith, choosing to go south rather than north. He had doubted for a while as to his immediate destination. The Altringhams were still at Castle Corry, and he might have received great comfort from her ladyship's advice and encouragement. But, intimate as he was with the Altringhams, he did not dare to take a liberty with the Earl. A certain allowance of splendid hospitality at Castle Corry was at his disposal every year, and Lord Altringham always welcomed him with thorough kindness. But George Hotspur had in some fashion been made to understand that he was not to overstay his time; and he was quite aware that the Earl could be very disagreeable upon occasions. There was a something in the Earl of which George was afraid; and, to tell the truth, he did not dare to go back to Castle Corry. And then, might it not be well for him to make immediate preparation in London for those inquiries respecting his debts and his character which Sir Harry had decided to make? It would be very difficult for him to make any preparation that could lead to a good result; but if no preparation were made, the result would be very bad indeed. It might perhaps be possible to do something with Mr. Hart and Captain Stubber. He had no other immediate engagements. In October he was due to shoot pheasants with a distinguished party in Norfolk, but this business which he had now in hand was of so much importance that even the pheasant-shooting and the distinguished party were not of much moment to him.

He went to Penrith, and thence direct to London. It was the habit of his life to give up his London lodgings when he left town at the end of the season, and spare himself the expense of any home as long as he could find friends to entertain him. There are certain items of the cost of living for which the greatest proficient in the art of tick must pay, or he will come to a speedy end;—and a man's lodging is one of them. If indeed the spendthrift adapts himself to the splendour of housekeeping, he may, provided his knowledge of his business be complete, and his courage adequate, house himself gloriously for a year or two with very small payment in ready money. He may even buy a mansion with an incredibly small outlay, and, when once in it, will not easily allow himself to be extruded. George Hotspur, however, not from any want of knowledge or of audacity, but from the nature of the life he chose to lead, had abstained from such investment of his credit, and had paid for his lodgings in St. James' Street. He was consequently houseless at the moment, and on his arrival in London took himself to a hotel close behind the military club to which he belonged.

At this moment he was comparatively a rich man. He had between three and four hundred pounds at a bank at which he kept an account when possessed of funds. But demands upon him were very pressing, and there was a certain Captain Stubber who was bitter against him, almost to blood, because one Mr. Abraham Hart had received two thousand pounds from the proceeds of Sir Harry's generosity. Captain Stubber had not received a shilling, and had already threatened Cousin George with absolute exposure if something were not done to satisfy him.

George, when he had ordered his dinner at his club, wrote the following letter to Lady Altringham. He had intended to write from Penrith in the morning, but when there had been out of sorts and unhappy, and had disliked to confess, after his note of triumph sounded on the previous evening, that he had been turned out of Humblethwaite. He had got over that feeling during the day, with the help of sundry glasses of sherry and a little mixed curaçoa and brandy which he took immediately on his arrival in London,—and, so supported, made a clean breast of it, as the reader shall see.

> DEAR LADY A., [he said]—
>
> Here I am, back in town, banished from heaven. My darling, gentle, future papa-in-law gave me to understand, when I told him the extent of my hopes last night, that the outside of the park-gates at Humblethwaite was the place for me; nevertheless he sent me to Penrith with the family horses, and, taking it as a whole, I think that my interview with him, although very disagreeable, was not unsatisfactory. I told him everything that I could tell him. He was kind enough to call me a blackguard (!!!) because I had gone to Emily without speaking to him first. On such occasions, however, a man takes anything. I ventured to suggest that what I had done was not unprecedented among young people, and hinted that while he could make me the future master of Humblethwaite, I could make my cousin the future Lady Hotspur; and that in no other way could Humblethwaite and the Hotspurs be kept together. It was wonderful how he cooled down after a while, saying that he would pay all my debts if he found them—satisfactory. I can only say that I never found them so.
>
> It ended in this—that he is to make inquiry about me, and that I am to have my cousin unless I am found out to be very bad indeed. How or when the inquiries will be made I do not know; but I am here to prepare for them.
>
> Yours always most faithfully,
>
> G. H.

> I do not like to ask Altringham to do anything for me. No man ever had a kinder friend than I have had in him, and I know he objects to meddle in the money matters of other people. But if he could lend me his name for a thousand pounds till I can get these things settled, I believe I could get over every other difficulty. I should as a matter of course include the amount in the list of debts which I should give to Sir Harry; but the sum at once, which I could raise on his name without trouble to him, would enable me to satisfy the only creditor who will be likely to do me real harm with Sir Harry. I think you will understand all this, and will perceive how very material the kindness to me may be; but if you think that Altringham will be unwilling to do it, you had better not show him this letter.

It was the mixed curaçoa and brandy which gave George Hotspur the courage to make the request contained in his postscript. He had not intended to make it when he sat down to write, but as he wrote the idea had struck him that if ever a man ought to use a friend this was an occasion for doing so. If he could get a thousand pounds from Lord Altringham, he might be able to stop Captain Stubber's mouth. He did not believe that he should be successful, and he thought it probable that Lord Altringham might express vehement displeasure. But the game was worth the candle, and then he knew that he could trust the Countess.

London was very empty, and he passed a wretched evening at his club. There were not men enough to make up a pool, and he was obliged to content himself with a game of billiards with an old half-pay naval captain, who never left London, and who would bet nothing beyond a shilling on the game. The half-pay navy captain won four games, thereby paying for his dinner, and then Cousin George went sulkily to bed.

He had come up to town expressly to see Captain Stubber and Mr. Hart, and perhaps also to see another friend from whom some advice might be had; but on the following morning he found himself very averse to seeking any of these advisers. He had applied to Lady Altringham for assistance, and he told himself that it would be wise to wait for her answer. And yet he knew that it would not be wise to wait, as Sir Harry would certainly be quick in making his promised inquiries. For four days he hung about between his hotel and his club, and then he got Lady Altringham's answer. We need only quote the passage which had reference to George's special request:—

> Gustavus says that he will have nothing to do with money. You know his feelings about it. And he says that it would do no good. Whatever the debts are, tell them plainly to Sir Harry. If this be some affair of play, as Gustavus supposes, tell that to Sir Harry. Gustavus thinks that the Baronet would without doubt pay any such debt which could be settled or partly settled by a thousand pounds.

"D——d heartless, selfish fellow! quite incapable of anything like true friendship," said Cousin George to himself, when he read Lady Altringham's letter.

Now he must do something. Hitherto neither Stubber, nor Hart, nor the other friend knew of his presence in London. Hart, though a Jew, was much less distasteful to him than Captain Stubber, and to Mr. Abraham Hart he went first.

Mr. Abraham Hart was an attorney,—so called by himself and friends,—living in a genteel street abutting on Gray's Inn Road, with whose residence and place of business, all beneath the same roof, George Hotspur was very well acquainted. Mr. Hart was a man in the prime of life, with black hair and a black beard, and a new shining hat, and a coat with a velvet collar and silk lining. He was always dressed in the same way, and had never yet been seen by Cousin George without his hat on his head. He was a pleasant-spoken, very ignorant, smiling, jocose man, with a slightly Jewish accent, who knew his business well, pursued it diligently, and considered himself to have a clear conscience. He had certain limits of forbearance with his customers—limits which were not narrow; but, when those were passed, he would sell the bed from under a dying woman with her babe, or bread from the mouth of a starving child. To do so was the necessity of his trade,—for his own guidance in which he had made laws. The breaking of those laws by himself would bring his trade to an end, and therefore he declined to break them.

Mr. Hart was a man who attended to his business, and he was found at home even in September. "Yes, Mr. 'Oshspur, it's about time something was done now; ain't it?" said Mr. Hart, smiling pleasantly.

Cousin George, also smiling, reminded his friend of the two thousand pounds paid to him only a few months since. "Not a shilling was mine of that, Captain 'Oshspur, not a brass fardin'. That was quite neshesshary just then, as you know, Captain 'Oshspur, or the fat must have been in the fire. And what's up now?"

Not without considerable difficulty Cousin George explained to the Jew gentleman what was "up." He probably assumed more inclination on the part of Sir Harry for the match than he was justified in doing; but was very urgent in explaining to Mr. Hart that when inquiry was made on the part of Sir Harry as to the nature of the debt, the naked truth should not be exactly told.

"It was very bad, vasn't it, Captain 'Oshspur, having to divide with that fellow Stubber the money from the 'Orse Guards? You vas too clever for both of us there, Mr. 'Oshspur; veren't you now, Captain 'Oshspur? And I've two cheques still on my 'ands which is marked 'No account!' 'No account' is very bad. Isn't 'No account' very bad on a cheque, Captain 'Oshspur? And then I've that cheque on Drummond, signed;—God knows how that is signed! There ain't no such person at all. Baldebeque! That's more like it than nothing else. When you brought me that, I thought there vas a Lord Baldebeque; and I know you live among lords, Captain 'Oshspur."

"On my honour I brought it you,—just as I took it at Tattersall's."

"There was an expert as I showed it to says it is your handwriting, Captain 'Oshspur."

"He lies!" said Cousin George, fiercely.

"But when Stubber would have half the sale money, for the commission—and wanted it all too! lord, how he did curse and swear! That was bad, Captain 'Oshspur."

Then Cousin George swallowed his fierceness for a time, and proceeded to explain to Mr. Hart that Sir Harry would certainly pay all his debts if only those little details could be kept back to which Mr. Hart had so pathetically alluded. Above all it would be necessary to preserve in obscurity that little mistake which had been made as to the pawning of the commission. Cousin George told a great many lies, but he told also much that was true. The Jew did not believe one of the lies; but then, neither did he believe much of the truth. When George had finished his story, then Mr. Hart had a story of his own to tell.

"To let you know all about it, Captain 'Oshspur, the old gent has begun about it already."

"What, Sir Harry?"

"Yes, Sir 'Arry. Mr. Boltby—"

"He's the family lawyer."

"I suppose so, Captain 'Oshspur. Vell, he vas here yesterday, and vas very polite. If I'd just tell him all about everything, he thought as 'ow the Baronet would settle the affair off 'and. He vas very generous in his offer, vas Mr. Boltby; but he didn't say nothin' of any marriage, Captain 'Oshspur."

"Of course he didn't. You are not such a fool as to suppose he would."

"No; I ain't such a fool as I looks, Captain Oshspur, am I? I didn't think it likely, seeing vat vas the nature of his interrogatories. Mr. Boltby seemed to know a good deal. It is astonishing how much them fellows do know."

"You didn't tell him anything?"

"Not much, Captain 'Oshspur—not at fust starting. I'm a going to have my money, you know, Captain 'Oshspur. And if I see my vay to my money one vay, and if I don't see no vay the other vay, vy, vhat's a man to do? You can't blame me, Captain 'Oshspur. I've been very indulgent with you; I have, Captain 'Oshspur."

Cousin George promised, threatened, explained, swore by all his gods, and ended by assuring Mr. Abraham Hart that his life and death were in that gentleman's keeping. If Mr. Hart would only not betray him, the money would be safe and the marriage would be safe, and everything would easily come right. Over and above other things, Cousin George would owe to Mr. Abraham Hart a debt of gratitude which never would be wholly paid. Mr. Hart could only say that he meant to have his money, but that he did not mean to be "ungenteel." Much in his opinion must depend on what Stubber would do. As for Stubber, he couldn't speak to Stubber himself, as he and Stubber "were two." As for himself, if he could get his money he certainly would not be "ungenteel." And he meant what he said—meant more than he said. He would still run some risk rather than split on an old customer such as "Captain 'Oshspur." But now that a sudden way to his money was opened to him, he could not undertake to lose sight of it.

With a very heavy heart Cousin George went from Mr. Hart's house to the house of call of Captain Stubber. Mr. Boltby had been before him with Hart, and he augured the worst from Sir Harry's activity in the matter. If Mr. Boltby had already seen the Captain, all his labour would probably be too late. Where Captain Stubber lived, even so old a friend of his as Cousin George did not know. And in what way Captain Stubber had become a captain, George, though he had been a military man himself, had never learned. But Captain Stubber had a house of call in a very narrow, dirty little street near Red Lion Square. It was close to a public-house, but did not belong to the public-house. George Hotspur, who had been very often to the place of call, had never seen there any appurtenances of the Captain's business. There were no account-books, no writing-table, no ink even, except that contained in a little box with a screw, which Captain Stubber would take out of his own pocket. Mr. Hart was so far established and civilized as to keep a boy whom he called a clerk; but Captain Stubber seemed to keep nothing. A dirty little girl at the house of call would run and fetch Captain Stubber, if he were within reach; but most usually an appointment had to be made with the Captain. Cousin George well remembered the day when his brother Captain first made his acquaintance. About two years after the commencement of his life in London, Captain Stubber had had an interview with him in the little waiting-room just within the club doors. Captain Stubber then had in his possession a trumpery note of hand with George's signature, which, as he stated, he had "done" for a small tradesman with whom George had been fool enough to deal for cigars. From that day to the present he and Captain Stubber had been upon most intimate and confidential terms. If there was any one in the world whom Cousin George really hated, it was Captain Stubber.

On this occasion Captain Stubber was forthcoming after a delay of about a quarter of an hour. During that time Cousin George had stood in the filthy little parlour of the house of call in a frame of mind which was certainly not to be envied. Had Mr. Boltby also been with Captain Stubber? He knew his two creditors well enough to understand that the Jew, getting his money, would be better pleased to serve him than to injure him. But the Captain would from choice do him an ill turn. Nothing but self-interest would tie up Captain Stubber's tongue. Captain Stubber was a tall thin gentleman, probably over sixty years of age, with very seedy clothes, and a red nose. He always had Berlin gloves, very much torn about the fingers, carried a cotton umbrella, wore—as his sole mark of respectability—a very stiff, clean, white collar round his neck, and invariably smelt of gin. No one knew where he lived, or how he carried on his business;

but, such as he was, he had dealings with large sums of money, or at least with bills professing to stand for large sums, and could never have been found without a case in his pocket crammed with these documents. The quarter of an hour seemed to George to be an age; but at last Captain Stubber knocked at the front door and was shown into the room.

"How d'ye do, Captain Stubber?" said George.

"I'd do a deal better, Captain Hotspur, if I found it easier sometimes to come by my own."

"Well, yes; but no doubt you have your profit in the delay, Captain Stubber."

"It's nothing to you, Captain Hotspur, whether I have profit or loss. All you 'as got to look to is to pay me what you owe me. And I intend that you shall, or by G—— you shall suffer for it! I'm not going to stand it any longer. I know where to have you, and have you I will."

Cousin George was not quite sure whether the Captain did know where to have him. If Mr. Boltby had been with him, it might be so; but then Captain Stubber was not a man so easily found as Mr. Hart, and the connection between himself and the Captain might possibly have escaped Mr. Boltby's inquiries. It was very difficult to tell the story of his love to such a man as Captain Stubber, but he did tell it. He explained all the difficulties of Sir Harry's position in regard to the title and the property, and he was diffuse upon his own advantages as head of the family, and of the need there was that he should marry the heiress.

"But there is not an acre of it will come to you unless he gives it you?" inquired Captain Stubber.

"Certainly not," said Cousin George, anxious that the Captain should understand the real facts of the case to a certain extent.

"And he needn't give you the girl?"

"The girl will give herself, my friend."

"And he needn't give the girl the property?"

"But he will. She is his only child."

"I don't believe a word about it. I don't believe such a one as Sir Harry Hotspur would lift his hand to help such as you."

"He has offered to pay my debts already."

"Very well. Let him make the offer to me. Look here, Captain Hotspur, I am not a bit afraid of you, you know."

"Who asks you to be afraid?"

"Of all the liars I ever met with, you are the worst."

George Hotspur smiled, looking up at the red nose of the malignant old man as though it were a joke; but that which he had to hear at this moment was a heavy burden. Captain Stubber probably understood this, for he repeated his words.

"I never knew any liar nigh so bad as you. And then there is such a deal worse than lies. I believe I could send you to penal servitude, Captain Hotspur."

"You could do no such thing," said Cousin George, still trying to look as though it were a joke, "and you don't think you could."

"I'll do my best at any rate, if I don't have my money soon. You could pay Mr. Hart two thousand pounds, but you think I'm nobody."

"I am making arrangements now for having every shilling paid to you."

"Yes, I see. I've known a good deal about your arrangements. Look here, Captain Hotspur, unless I have five hundred pounds on or before Saturday, I'll write to Sir Harry Hotspur, and I'll give him a statement of all our dealings. You can trust me, though I can't trust you. Good morning, Captain Hotspur."

Captain Stubber did believe in his heart that he was a man much injured by Cousin George, and that Cousin George was one whom he was entitled to despise. And yet a poor wretch more despicable, more dishonest, more false, more wicked, or more cruel than Captain Stubber could not have been found in all London. His business was carried on with a small capital borrowed from a firm of low attorneys, who were the real holders of the bills he carried, and the profits which they allowed him to make were very trifling. But from Cousin George during the last twelve months he had made no profit at all. And Cousin George in former days had trodden upon him as on a worm.

Cousin George did not fail to perceive that Mr. Boltby had not as yet applied to Captain Stubber.

Chapter XI.

Mrs. Morton.

Five hundred pounds before Saturday, and this was Tuesday! As Cousin George was taken westward from Red Lion Square in a cab, three or four different lines of conduct suggested themselves to him. In the first place, it would be a very good thing to murder Captain Stubber. In the present effeminate state of civilization and with the existing scruples as to the value of human life, he did not see his way clearly in this direction, but entertained the project rather as a beautiful castle in the air. The two next suggestions were to pay him the money demanded, or to pay him half of it. The second suggestion was the simpler, as the state of Cousin George's funds made it feasible; but then that brute would probably refuse to take the half in lieu of the whole when he found that his demand had absolutely produced a tender of ready cash. As for paying the whole, it might perhaps be done. It was still possible that, with such prospects before him as those he now possessed, he could raise a hundred or hundred and fifty pounds; but then he would be left penniless. The last course of action which he contemplated was, to take no further notice of Captain Stubber, and let him tell his story to Sir Harry if he chose to tell it. The

man was such a blackguard that his entire story would probably
not be believed; and then was it not almost necessary that Sir
Harry should hear it? Of course there would be anger, and
reproaches, and threats, and difficulty. But if Emily would be
true to him, they might all by degrees be levelled down. This
latter line of conduct would be practicable, and had this beautiful
attraction,—that it would save for his own present use that
charming balance of ready money which he still possessed. Had
Altringham possessed any true backbone of friendship, he might
now, he thought, have been triumphant over all his difficulties.

When he sat down to his solitary dinner at his club, he
was very tired with his day's work. Attending to the affairs of
such gentlemen as Mr. Hart and Captain Stubber,—who well
know how to be masterful when their time for being masterful
has come,—is fatiguing enough. But he had another task to
perform before he went to bed, which he would fain have kept
unperformed were it possible to do so. He had written to a third
friend to make an appointment for the evening, and this
appointment he was bound to keep. He would very much rather
have stayed at his club and played billiards with the navy
captain, even though he might again have lost his shillings. The
third friend was that Mrs. Morton to whom Lord Altringham had
once alluded. "I supposed that it was coming," said Mrs.
Morton, when she had listened, without letting a word fall from
her own lips, to the long rambling story which Cousin George
told her,—a rambling story in which there were many lies, but in
which there was the essential truth, that Cousin George intended,
if other things could be made to fit, to marry his cousin Emily
Hotspur. Mrs. Morton was a woman who had been handsome,—
dark, thin, with great brown eyes and thin lips and a long well-
formed nose; she was in truth three years younger than George
Hotspur, but she looked to be older. She was a clever woman
and well read too, and in every respect superior to the man
whom she had condescended to love. She earned her bread by
her profession as an actress, and had done so since her earliest

years. What story there may be of a Mr. Morton who had years ago married, and ill-used, and deserted her, need not here be told. Her strongest passion at this moment was love for the cold-blooded reprobate who had now come to tell her of his intended marriage. She had indeed loved George Hotspur, and George had been sufficiently attached to her to condescend to take aid from her earnings.

"I supposed that it was coming," she said in a low voice when he brought to an end the rambling story which she had allowed him to tell without a word of interruption.

"What is a fellow to do?" said George.

"Is she handsome?"

George thought that he might mitigate the pain by making little of his cousin. "Well, no, not particularly. She looks like a lady."

"And I suppose I don't." For a moment there was a virulence in this which made poor George almost gasp. This woman was patient to a marvel, long-bearing, affectionate, imbued with that conviction so common to woman and the cause of so much delight to men,—that ill-usage and suffering are intended for woman; but George knew that she could turn upon him if goaded far enough, and rend him. He could depend upon her for very much, because she loved him; but he was afraid of her. "You didn't mean that, I know," she added, smiling.

"Of course I didn't."

"No; your cruelties don't lie in that line; do they, George?"

"I'm sure I never mean to be cruel to you, Lucy."

"I don't think you do. I hardly believe that you ever mean anything,—except just to get along and live."

"A fellow must live, you know," said George.

In ordinary society George Hotspur could be bright, and he was proud of being bright. With this woman he was always subdued, always made to play second fiddle, always talked like a boy; and he knew it. He had loved her once, if he was capable of loving anything; but her mastery over him wearied him, even though he was, after a fashion, proud of her cleverness, and he wished that she were,—well, dead, if the reader choose that mode of expressing what probably were George's wishes. But he had never told himself that he desired her death. He could build pleasant castles in the air as to the murder of Captain Stubber, but his thoughts did not travel that way in reference to Mrs. Morton.

"She is not pretty, then,—this rich bride of yours?"

"Not particularly; she's well enough, you know."

"And well enough is good enough for you;—is it? Do you love her, George?"

The woman's voice was very low and plaintive as she asked the question. Though from moment to moment she could use her little skill in pricking him with her satire, still she loved him; and she would vary her tone, and as at one minute she would make him uneasy by her raillery, so at the next she would quell him by her tenderness. She looked into his face for a reply, when he hesitated. "Tell me that you do not love her," she said, passionately.

"Not particularly," replied George.

"And yet you would marry her?"

"What's a fellow to do? You see how I am fixed about the title. These are kinds of things to which a man situated as I am is obliged to submit."

"Royal obligations, as one might call them."

"By George, yes," said George, altogether missing the satire. From any other lips he would have been sharp enough to catch it. "One can't see the whole thing go to the dogs after it has kept its head up so long! And then you know, a man can't live altogether without an income."

"You have done so, pretty well."

"I know that I owe you a lot of money, Lucy; and I know also that I mean to pay you."

"Don't talk about that. I don't know how at such a time as this you can bring yourself to mention it." Then she rose from her seat and flashed into wrath, carried on by the spirit of her own words. "Look here, George; if you send me any of that woman's money, by the living God I will send it back to herself. To buy me with her money! But it is so like a man."

"I didn't mean that. Sir Harry is to pay all my debts."

"And will not that be the same? Will it not be her money? Why is he to pay your debts? Because he loves you?"

"It is all a family arrangement. You don't quite understand."

"Of course I don't understand. Such a one as I cannot lift myself so high above the earth. Great families form a sort of heaven of their own, which poor broken, ill-conditioned, wretched, common creatures such as I am cannot hope to comprehend. But, by heaven, what a lot of the vilest clay goes to the making of that garden of Eden! Look here, George;—you have nothing of your own?"

"Not much, indeed."

"Nothing. Is not that so? You can answer me at any rate."

"You know all about it," he said,—truly enough, for she did know.

"And you cannot earn a penny."

"I don't know that I can. I never was very good at earning anything."

"It isn't gentlemanlike, is it? But I can earn money."

"By George! yes. I've often envied you. I have indeed."

"How flattering! As far as it went you should have had it all,—nearly all,—if you could have been true to me."

"But, Lucy,—about the family?"

"And about your debts? Of course I couldn't pay debts which were always increasing. And of course your promises for the future were false. We both knew that they were false when they were made. Did we not?" She paused for an answer, but he made none. "They meant nothing; did they? He is dead now."

"Morton is dead?"

"Yes; he died in San Francisco, months ago."

"I couldn't have known that, Lucy; could I?"

"Don't be a fool! What difference would it have made? Don't pretend anything so false. It would be disgusting on the very face of it. It mattered nothing to you whether he lived or died. When is it to be?"

"When is what to be?"

"Your marriage with this ill-looking young woman, who has got money, but whom you do not even pretend to love."

It struck even George that this was a way in which Emily Hotspur should not be described. She had been acknowledged to be the beauty of the last season, one of the finest girls that had ever been seen about London; and, as for loving her,—he did love her. A man might be fond of two dogs, or have two pet horses, and why shouldn't he love two women! Of course he loved his cousin. But his circumstances at the moment were difficult, and he didn't quite know how to explain all this.

"When is it to be?" she said, urging her question imperiously.

In answer to this he gave her to understand that there was still a good deal of difficulty. He told her something of his position with Captain Stubber, and defined,—not with absolute correctness,—the amount of consent which Sir Harry had given to the marriage.

"And what am I to do?" she asked.

He looked blankly into her face. She then rose again, and unlocking a desk with a key that hung at her girdle, she took from it a bundle of papers.

"There," she said; "there is the letter in which I have your promise to marry me when I am free;—as I am now. It could not be less injurious to you than when locked up there; but the remembrance of it might frighten you." She threw the letter to him across the table, but he did not touch it. "And here are others which might be taken to mean the same thing. There! I am

not so injured as I might seem to be,—for I never believed them.
How could I believe anything that you would say to me,—
anything that you would write?"

"Don't be down on me too hard, Lucy."

"No, I will not be down upon you at all. If these things
pained you, I would not say them. Shall I destroy the letters?"
Then she took them, one after another, and tore them into small
fragments. "You will be easier now, I know."

"Easy! I am not very easy, I can tell you."

"Captain Stubber will not let you off so gently as I do. Is
that it?"

Then there was made between them a certain pecuniary
arrangement, which if Mrs. Morton trusted at all the undertaking
made to her, showed a most wonderful faith on her part. She
would lend him £250 towards the present satisfaction of Captain
Stubber; and this sum, to be lent for such a purpose, she would
consent to receive back again out of Sir Harry's money. She
must see a certain manager, she said; but she did not doubt but
that her loan would be forthcoming on the Saturday morning.
Captain George Hotspur accepted the offer, and was profuse in
his thanks. After that, when he was going, her weakness was
almost equal to his vileness.

"You will come and see me," she said, as she held his
hand. Again he paused a moment. "George, you will come and
see me?"

"Oh, of course I will."

"A great deal I can bear; a great deal I have borne; but do
not be a coward. I knew you before she did, and have loved you
better, and have treated you better than ever she will do. Of
course you will come?"

He promised her that he would, and then went from her.

On the Saturday morning Captain Stubber was made
temporarily happy by the most unexpected receipt of five
hundred pounds.

Chapter XII.

The Hunt Becomes Hot.

September passed away with Captain Hotspur very unpleasantly. He had various interviews with Captain Stubber, with Mr. Hart, and with other creditors, and found very little amusement. Lady Altringham had written to him again, advising him strongly to make out a complete list of his debts, and to send them boldly to Sir Harry. He endeavoured to make out the list, but had hardly the audacity to do it even for his own information. When the end of September had come, and he was preparing himself to join the party of distinguished pheasant-shooters in Norfolk, he had as yet sent no list to Sir Harry, nor had he heard a word from Humblethwaite. Certain indications had reached him,—continued to reach him from day to day,— that Mr. Boltby was at work, but no communication had been made actually to himself even by Mr. Boltby. When and how and in what form he was expected to send the schedule of his debts to Sir Harry he did not know; and thus it came to pass that when the time came for his departure from town, he had sent no such schedule at all. His sojourn, however, with the distinguished party was to last only for a week, and then he would really go to work. He would certainly himself write to Sir Harry before the end of October.

In the meantime there came other troubles,—various other troubles. One other trouble vexed him sore. There came to him a note from a gentleman with whom his acquaintance was familiar though slight,—as follows:—

DEAR HOTSPUR,—

Did I not meet you at the last Goodwood meeting? If you don't mind, pray answer me the question. You will remember, I do not doubt, that I did; that I lost my money too, and paid it.

—Yours ever,

F. STACKPOOLE.

He understood it all immediately. The Stackpooles had been at Humblethwaite. But what business had the man to write letters to him with the object of getting him into trouble? He did not answer the note, but, nevertheless, it annoyed him much. And then there was another great vexation. He was now running low in funds for present use. He had made what he feared was a most useless outlay in satisfying Stubber's immediate greed for money, and the effect was, that at the beginning of the last week in September he found himself with hardly more than fifty sovereigns in his possession, which would be considerably reduced before he could leave town. He had been worse off before,—very much worse; but it was especially incumbent on him now to keep up that look of high feather which cannot be maintained in its proper brightness without ready cash. He must take a man-servant with him among the distinguished guests; he must fee gamekeepers, pay railway fares, and have loose cash about him for a hundred purposes. He wished it to be known that he was going to marry his cousin. He might find some friend with softer heart than Altringham, who would lend him a few hundreds on being made to believe in this brilliant destiny; but a roll of bank-notes in his pocket would greatly aid him in making the destiny credible. Fifty pounds, as he well knew, would melt away from him like snow. The last fifty pounds of a thousand always goes quicker than any of the nineteen other fifties.

Circumstances had made it impossible for him to attend the Leger this year, but he had put a little money on it. The result had done nothing for or against him,—except this, that whereas he received between one and two hundred pounds, he conceived the idea of paying only a portion of what he had lost. With reference to the remainder, he wrote to ask his friend if it would be quite the same if the money were paid at Christmas. If not, of course it should be sent at once. The friend was one of the Altringham set, who had been at Castle Corry, and who had heard of George's hopes in reference to his cousin. George added a postscript to his letter: "This kind of thing will be over for me very soon. I am to be a Benedict, and the house of Humblethwaite and the title are to be kept together. I know you will congratulate me. My cousin is a charming girl, and worth all that I shall lose ten times over." It was impossible, he thought, that the man should refuse him credit for eighty pounds till Christmas, when the man should know that he was engaged to be married to £20,000 a year! But the man did refuse. The man wrote back to say that he did not understand this kind of thing at all, and that he wanted his money at once. George Hotspur sent the man his money, not without many curses on the illiberality of such a curmudgeon. Was it not cruel that a fellow would not give him so trifling an assistance when he wanted it so badly? All the world seemed to conspire to hurt him just at this most critical moment of his life! In many of his hardest emergencies for ready money he had gone to Mrs. Morton. But even he felt that just at present he could not ask her for more.

Nevertheless, a certain amount of cash was made to be forthcoming before he took his departure for Norfolk. In the course of the preceding spring he had met a young gentleman in Mr. Hart's small front parlour, who was there upon ordinary business. He was a young gentleman with good prospects, and with some command of ready money; but he liked to live, and would sometimes want Mr. Hart's assistance. His name was Walker, and though he was not exactly one of that class in which it delighted Captain Hotspur to move, nevertheless he was not altogether disdained by that well-born and well-bred gentleman. On the third of October, the day before he left London to join his distinguished friends in Norfolk, George Hotspur changed a cheque for nearly three hundred pounds at Mr. Walker's banker's. Poor Mr. Walker! But Cousin George went down to Norfolk altogether in high feather. If there were play, he would play. He would bet about pulling straws if he could find an adversary to bet with him. He could chink sovereigns about at his ease, at any rate, during the week. Cousin George liked to chink sovereigns about at his ease. And this point of greatness must be conceded to him,—that, however black might loom the clouds of the coming sky, he could enjoy the sunshine of the hour.

In the meantime Mr. Boltby was at work, and before Cousin George had shot his last pheasant in such very good company, Sir Harry was up in town assisting Mr. Boltby. How things had gone at Humblethwaite between Sir Harry and his daughter must not be told on this page; but the reader may understand that nothing had as yet occurred to lessen Sir Harry's objection to the match. There had been some correspondence between Sir Harry and Mr. Boltby, and Sir Harry had come up to town. When the reader learns that on the very day on which Cousin George and his servant were returning to London by the express train from Norfolk, smoking many cigars and drinking many glasses,—George of sherry, and the servant probably of beer and spirits alternately,—each making himself happy with a novel; George's novel being French, and that of the servant English sensational,—the reader, when he learns that on this very day Sir Harry had interviews with Captain Stubber and also with Mrs. Morton, will be disposed to think that things were not going very well for Cousin George. But then the reader does not as yet know the nature of the persistency of Emily Hotspur.

What Sir Harry did with Captain Stubber need not be minutely described. There can be no doubt that Cousin George was not spared by the Captain, and that when he understood what might be the result of telling the truth, he told all that he knew. In that matter of the £500 Cousin George had really been ill-treated. The payment had done him no sort of service whatever. Of Captain Stubber's interview with Sir Harry nothing further need now be said. But it must be explained that Sir Harry, led astray by defective information, made a mistake in regard to Mrs. Morton, and found out his mistake. He did not much like Mrs. Morton, but he did not leave her without an ample apology. From Mrs. Morton he learned nothing whatever in regard to Cousin George,—nothing but this, that Mrs. Morton did not deny that she was acquainted with Captain Hotspur. Mr. Boltby had learned, however, that Cousin George had drawn the money for a cheque payable to her order, and he had made himself nearly certain of the very nature of the transaction.

Early on the morning after George's return he was run to ground by Mr. Boltby's confidential clerk, at the hotel behind the club. It was so early, to George at least, that he was still in bed. But the clerk, who had breakfasted at eight, been at his office by nine, and had worked hard for two hours and a half since, did not think it at all early. George, who knew that his pheasant-shooting pleasure was past, and that immediate trouble was in store for him, had consoled himself over-night with a good deal of curaçoa and seltzer and brandy, and had taken these comforting potations after a bottle of champagne. He was, consequently, rather out of sorts when he was run to ground in his very bedroom by Boltby's clerk. He was cantankerous at first, and told the clerk to go and be d——d. The clerk pleaded Sir Harry. Sir Harry was in town, and wanted to see his cousin. A meeting must, of course, be arranged. Sir Harry wished that it might be in Mr. Boltby's private room. When Cousin George objected that he did not choose to have any interview with Sir Harry in presence of the lawyer, the clerk very humbly explained that the private room would be exclusively for the service of the two gentlemen. Sick as he was, Cousin George knew that nothing was to be gained by quarrelling with Sir Harry. Though Sir Harry should ask for an interview in presence of the Lord Mayor, he must go to it. He made the hour as late as he could, and at last three o'clock was settled.

At one, Cousin George was at work upon his broiled bones and tea laced with brandy, having begun his meal with soda and brandy. He was altogether dissatisfied with himself. Had he known on the preceding evening what was coming, he would have dined on a mutton chop and a pint of sherry, and have gone to bed at ten o'clock. He looked at himself in the glass, and saw that he was bloated and red,—and a thing foul to behold. It was a matter of boast to him,—the most pernicious boast that ever a man made,—that in twenty-four hours he could rid himself of all outward and inward sign of any special dissipation; but the twenty-four hours were needed, and now not twelve were allowed him. Nevertheless, he kept his appointment. He tried to invent some lie which he might send by a commissioner, and which might not ruin him. But he thought upon the whole that it would be safer for him to go.

When he entered the room he saw at a glance that there was to be war,—war to the knife,—between him and Sir Harry. He perceived at once that if it were worth his while to go on with the thing at all, he must do so in sole dependence on the spirit and love of Emily Hotspur. Sir Harry at their first greeting declined to shake hands with him, and called him Captain Hotspur.

"Captain Hotspur," he said, "in a word, understand that there must be no further question of a marriage between you and my daughter."

"Why not, Sir Harry?"

"Because, sir—" and then he paused—"I would sooner see my girl dead at my feet than entrust her to such a one as you. It was true what you said to me at Humblethwaite. There would have been something very alluring to me in the idea of joining the property and the title together. A man will pay much for such a whim. I would not unwillingly have paid very much in money; but I am not so infamously wicked as to sacrifice my daughter utterly by giving her to one so utterly unworthy of her as you are."

"I told you that I was in debt, Sir Harry."

"I wanted no telling as to that; but I did want telling as to your mode of life, and I have had it now. You had better not press me. You had better see Mr. Boltby. He will tell you what I am willing to do for you upon receiving your written assurance that you will never renew your offer of marriage to Miss Hotspur."

"I cannot do that," said Cousin George, hoarsely.

"Then I shall leave you with your creditors to deal with as they please. I have nothing further to suggest myself, and I would recommend that you should see Mr. Boltby before you leave the chambers."

"What does my cousin say?" he asked.

"Were you at Goodwood last meeting?" asked Sir Harry. "But of course you were."

"I was," he answered. He was obliged to acknowledge so much, not quite knowing what Stackpoole might have said or done. "But I can explain that."

"There is no need whatever of any explanation. Do you generally borrow money from such ladies as Mrs. Morton?" Cousin George blushed when this question was asked, but made no answer to it. It was one that he could not answer. "But it makes no difference, Captain Hotspur. I mention these things only to let you feel that I know you. I must decline any further speech with you. I strongly advise you to see Mr. Boltby at once. Good afternoon."

So saying, the Baronet withdrew quickly, and Cousin George heard him shut the door of the chambers.

After considering the matter for a quarter of an hour, Cousin George made up his mind that he would see the lawyer. No harm could come to him from seeing the lawyer. He was closeted with Mr. Boltby for nearly an hour, and before he left the chamber had been forced to confess to things of which he had not thought it possible that Mr. Boltby should ever have heard. Mr. Boltby knew the whole story of the money raised on the commission, of the liabilities to both Hart and Stubber, and had acquainted himself with the history of Lord Baldebeque's cheque. Mr. Boltby was not indignant, as had been Sir Harry, but intimated it as a thing beyond dispute that a man who had done such things as could be proved against Cousin George,—and as would undoubtedly be proved against him if he would not give up his pursuit of the heiress,—must be disposed of with severity, unless he retreated at once of his own accord. Mr. Boltby did indeed hint something about a criminal prosecution, and utter ruin, and—incarceration.

But if George Hotspur would renounce his cousin utterly,—putting his renunciation on paper,—Sir Harry would pay all his debts to the extent of twenty thousand pounds, would allow him four hundred a year on condition that he would live out of England, and would leave him a further sum of twenty thousand pounds by his will, on condition that no renewed cause of offence were given.

"You had better, perhaps, go home and think about it, Mr. Hotspur," said the lawyer. Cousin George did go away and think about it.

Chapter XIII.

"I Will Not Desert Him."

Sir Harry, before he had left Humblethwaite for London in October, had heard enough of his cousin's sins to make him sure that the match must be opposed with all his authority. Indeed he had so felt from the first moment in which George had begun to tell him of what had occurred at Airey Force. He had never thought that George Hotspur would make a fitting husband for his daughter. But, without so thinking, he had allowed his mind to dwell upon the outside advantages of the connection, dreaming of a fitness which he knew did not exist, till he had vacillated, and the evil thing had come upon him. When the danger was so close upon him to make him see what it was, to force him to feel what would be the misery threatened to his daughter, to teach him to realize his own duty, he condemned himself bitterly for his own weakness. Could any duty which he owed to the world be so high or so holy as that which was due from him to his child? He almost hated his name and title and position as he thought of the evil that he had already done. Had his cousin George been in no close succession to the title, would he have admitted a man of whom he knew so much ill, and of whom he had never heard any good, within his park palings?

And then he could not but acknowledge to himself that by asking such a one to his house,—a man such as this young cousin who was known to be the heir to the title,—he had given his daughter special reason to suppose that she might regard him as a fitting suitor for her hand. She of course had known,—had felt as keenly as he had felt, for was she not a Hotspur?—that she would be true to her family by combining her property and the title, and that by yielding to such a marriage she would be doing a family duty, unless there were reasons against it stronger than those connected with his name. But as to those other reasons, must not her father and her mother know better than she could know? When she found that the man was made welcome both in town and country, was it not natural that she should suppose that there were no stronger reasons? All this Sir Harry felt, and blamed himself and determined that though he must oppose his daughter and make her understand that the hope of such a marriage must be absolutely abandoned, it would be his duty to be very tender with her. He had sinned against her already, in that he had vacillated and had allowed that handsome but vile and worthless cousin to come near her.

In his conduct to his daughter, Sir Harry endeavoured to be just, and tender, and affectionate; but in his conduct to his wife on the occasion he allowed himself some scope for the ill-humour not unnaturally incident to his misfortune. "Why on earth you should have had him in Bruton Street when you knew very well what he was, I cannot conceive," said Sir Harry.

"But I didn't know," said Lady Elizabeth, fearing to remind her husband that he also had sanctioned the coming of the cousin.

"I had told you. It was there that the evil was done. And then to let them go to that picnic together!"

"What could I do when Mrs. Fitzpatrick asked to be taken? You wouldn't have had me tell Emily that she should not be one of the party."

"I would have put it off till he was out of the house."

"But the Fitzpatricks were going too," pleaded the poor woman.

"It wouldn't have happened at all if you had not asked him to stay till the Monday," said Sir Harry; and to this charge Lady Elizabeth knew that there was no answer. There she had clearly disobeyed her husband; and though she doubtless suffered much from some dim idea of injustice, she was aware that as she had so offended she must submit to be told that all this evil had come from her wrong-doing.

"I hope she will not be obstinate," said Sir Harry to his wife. Lady Elizabeth, though she was not an acute judge of character, did know her own daughter, and was afraid to say that Emily would not be obstinate. She had the strongest possible respect as well as affection for her own child; she thoroughly believed in Emily—much more thoroughly than she did in herself. But she could not say that in such a matter Emily would not be obstinate. Lady Elizabeth was very intimately connected with two obstinate persons, one of whom was young and the other old; and she thought that perhaps the younger was the more obstinate of the two.

"It is quite out of the question that she should marry him," said Sir Harry, sadly. Still Lady Elizabeth made no reply. "I do not think that she will disobey me," continued Sir Harry. Still Lady Elizabeth said nothing. "If she gives me a promise, she will keep it," said Sir Harry.

Then the mother could answer, "I am sure she will."

"If the worst come to the worst, we must go away."

"To Scarrowby?" suggested Lady Elizabeth, who hated Scarrowby.

"That would do no good. Scarrowby would be the same as Humblethwaite to her, or perhaps worse. I mean abroad. We must shut up the place for a couple of years, and take her to Naples and Vienna, or perhaps to Egypt. Everything must be changed to her!—that is, if the evil has gone deep enough."

"Is he so very bad?" asked Lady Elizabeth.

"He is a liar and a blackguard, and I believe him to be a swindler," said Sir Harry. Then Lady Elizabeth was mute, and her husband left her.

At this time he had heard the whole story of the pawning of the commission, had been told something of money raised by worthless cheques, and had run to ground that lie about the Goodwood races. But he had not yet heard anything special of Mrs. Morton. The only attack on George's character which had as yet been made in the hearing of Emily had been with reference to the Goodwood races. Mrs. Stackpoole was a lady of some determination, and one who in society liked to show that she was right in her assertions, and well informed on matters in dispute; and she hated Cousin George. There had therefore come to be a good deal said about the Goodwood meeting, so that the affair reached Sir Harry's ears. He perceived that Cousin George had lied, and determined that Emily should be made to know that her cousin had lied. But it was very difficult to persuade her of this. That everybody else should tell stories about George and the Goodwood meeting seemed to her to be natural enough; she contented herself with thinking all manner of evil of Mr. and Mrs. Stackpoole, and reiterating her conviction that George Hotspur had not been at the meeting in question.

"I don't know that it much signifies," Mrs. Stackpoole had said in anger.

"Not in the least," Emily had replied, "only that I happen to know that my cousin was not there. He goes to so many race meetings that there has been some little mistake."

Then Mr. Stackpoole had written to Cousin George, and Cousin George had thought it wise to make no reply. Sir Harry, however, from other sources had convinced himself of the truth, and had told his daughter that there was evidence enough to prove the fact in any court of law. Emily when so informed had simply held her tongue, and had resolved to hate Mrs. Stackpoole worse than ever.

She had been told from the first that her engagement with her cousin would not receive her father's sanction; and for some days after that there had been silence on the subject at Humblethwaite, while the correspondence with Mr. Boltby was being continued. Then there came the moment in which Sir Harry felt that he must call upon his daughter to promise obedience, and the conversation which has been described between him and Lady Elizabeth was preparatory to his doing so.

"My dear," he said to his daughter, "sit down; I want to speak to you."

He had sent for her into his own morning room, in which she did not remember to have been asked to sit down before. She would often visit him there, coming in and out on all manner of small occasions, suggesting that he should ride with her, asking for the loan of a gardener for a week for some project of her own, telling him of a big gooseberry, interrupting him ruthlessly on any trifle in the world. But on such occasions she would stand close to him, leaning on him. And he would scold her,— playfully, or kiss her, or bid her begone from the room,—but would always grant what she asked of him. To him, though he hardly knew that it was so, such visits from his darling had been the bright moments of his life. But up to this morning he had never bade her be seated in that room.

"Emily," he said, "I hope you understand that all this about your cousin George must be given up." She made no reply, though he waited perhaps for a minute. "It is altogether out of the question. I am very, very sorry that you have been subjected to such a sorrow. I will own that I have been to blame for letting him come to my house."

"No, Papa, no."

"Yes, my dear, I have been to blame, and I feel it keenly. I did not then know as much of him as I do now, but I had heard that which should have made me careful to keep him out of your company."

"Hearing about people, Papa! Is that fair? Are we not always hearing tales about everybody?"

"My dear child, you must take my word for something."

"I will take it for everything in all the world, Papa."

"He has been a thoroughly bad young man."

"But, Papa—"

"You must take my word for it when I tell you that I have positive proof of what I am telling you."

"But, Papa—"

"Is not that enough?"

"No, Papa. I am heartily sorry that he should have been what you call a bad young man. I wish young men weren't so bad;—that there were no racecourses, and betting, and all that. But if he had been my brother instead of my cousin—"

"Don't talk about your brother, Emily."

"Should we hate him because he has been unsteady? Should we not do all that we could in the world to bring him back? I do not know that we are to hate people because they do what they ought not to do."

"We hate liars."

"He is not a liar. I will not believe it."

"Why did he tell you that he was not at those races, when he was there as surely as you are here? But, my dear, I will not argue about all this with you. It is not right that I should do so. It is my duty to inquire into these things, and yours to believe me and to obey me." Then he paused, but his daughter made no reply to him. He looked into her face, and saw there that mark about her eyes which he knew he so often showed himself; which he so well remembered with his father. "I suppose you do believe me, Emily, when I tell you that he is worthless."

"He need not be worthless always."

"His conduct has been such that he is unfit to be trusted with anything."

"He must be the head of our family some day, Papa."

"That is our misfortune, my dear. No one can feel it as I do. But I need not add to it the much greater misfortune of sacrificing to him my only child."

"If he was so bad, why did he come here?"

"That is true. I did not expect to be rebuked by you, Emily, but I am open to that rebuke."

"Dear, dear Papa, indeed I did not mean to rebuke you. But I cannot give him up."

"You must give him up."

"No, Papa. If I did, I should be false. I will not be false. You say that he is false. I do not know that, but I will not be false. Let me speak to you for one minute."

"It is of no use."

"But you will hear me, Papa. You always hear me when I speak to you." She had left her chair now, and was standing close to him, not leaning upon him as was her wont in their pleasantest moments of fellowship, but ready to do so whenever she should find that his mood would permit it. "I will never marry him without your leave."

"Thanks, Emily; I know how sacred is a promise from you."

"But mine to him is equally sacred. I shall still be engaged to him. I told him how it would be. I said that, as long as you or Mamma lived, I would never marry without your leave. Nor would I see him, or write to him without your knowledge. I told him so. But I told him also that I would always be true to him. I mean to keep my word."

"If you find him to be utterly worthless, you cannot be bound by such a promise."

"I hope it may not be so. I do not believe that it is so. I know him too well to think that he can be utterly worthless. But if he was, who should try to save him from worthlessness if not his nearest relatives? We try to reclaim the worst criminals, and sometimes we succeed. And he must be the head of the family.

Remember that. Ought we not to try to reclaim him? He cannot be worse than the prodigal son."

"He is ten times worse. I cannot tell you what has been his life."

"Papa, I have often thought that in our rank of life society is responsible for the kind of things which young men do. If he was at Goodwood, which I do not believe, so was Mr. Stackpoole. If he was betting, so was Mr. Stackpoole."

"But Mr. Stackpoole did not lie."

"I don't know that," she said, with a little toss of her head.

"Emily, you have no business either to say or to think it."

"I care nothing for Mr. Stackpoole whether he tells truth or not. He and his wife have made themselves very disagreeable,—that is all. But as for George, he is what he is, because other young men are allowed to be the same."

"You do not know the half of it."

"I know as much as I want to know, Papa. Let one keep as clear of it as one can, it is impossible not to hear how young men live. And yet they are allowed to go everywhere, and are flattered and encouraged. I do not pretend that George is better than others. I wish he were. Oh, how I wish it! But such as he is he belongs in a way to us, and we ought not to desert him. He belongs, I know, to me, and I will not desert him."

Sir Harry felt that there was no arguing with such a girl as this. Some time since he had told her that it was unfit that he should be brought into an argument with his own child, and there was nothing now for him but to fall back upon the security which that assertion gave him. He could not charge her with direct disobedience, because she had promised him that she would not do any of those things which, as a father, he had a right to forbid. He relied fully on her promise, and so far might feel himself to be safe. Nevertheless he was very unhappy. Of what service would his child be to him or he to her, if he were doomed to see her pining from day to day with an unpermitted love? It was the dearest wish of his heart to make her happy, as it was his fondest ambition to see her so placed in the world that she might be the happy transmitter of all the honours of the house of Humblethwaite,—if she could not transmit all the honours of the name. Time might help him. And then if she could be made really to see how base was the clay of which had been made this image which she believed to be of gold, might it not be that at last she would hate a thing that was so vile? In order that she might do so, he would persist in finding out what had been the circumstances of this young man's life. If, as he believed, the things which George Hotspur had done were such as in another rank of life would send the perpetrator to the treadmill, surely then she would not cling to her lover. It would not be in her nature to prefer that which was foul and abominable and despised of all men. It was after this, when he had seen Mr. Boltby, that the idea occurred to him of buying up Cousin George, so that Cousin George should himself abandon his engagement.

"You had better go now, my dear," he said, after his last speech. "I fully rely upon the promise you have made me. I know that I can rely upon it. And you also may rely upon me. I give you my word as your father that this man is unfit to be your husband, and that I should commit a sin greater than I can describe to you were I to give my sanction to such a marriage."

Emily made no answer to this, but left the room without having once leaned upon her father's shoulder.

That look of hers troubled him sadly when he was alone. What was to be the meaning of it, and what the result? She had given him almost unasked the only promise which duty required her to give, but at the same time she had assured him by her countenance, as well as by her words, that she would be as faithful to her lover as she was prepared to be obedient to her father. And then if there should come a long contest of that nature, and if he should see her devoted year after year to a love which she would not even try to cast off from her, how would he be able to bear it? He, too, was firm, but he knew himself to be as tender-hearted as he was obstinate. It would be more than he could bear. All the world would be nothing for him then. And if there were ever to be a question of yielding, it would be easier to do something towards lessening the vileness of the man now than hereafter. He, too, had some of that knowledge of the world which had taught Lady Altringham to say that the young people in such contests could always beat the old people. Thinking of this, and of that look upon his child's brows, he almost vacillated again. Any amount of dissipation he could now have forgiven; but to be a liar, too, and a swindler! Before he went to bed that night he had made up his mind to go to London and to see Mr. Boltby.

Chapter XIV.

Pertinacity.

On the day but one after the scene narrated in the last chapter Sir Harry went to London, and Lady Elizabeth and Emily were left alone together in the great house at Humblethwaite. Emily loved her mother dearly. The proper relations of life were reversed between them, and the younger domineered over the elder. But the love which the daughter felt was probably the stronger on this account. Lady Elizabeth never scolded, never snubbed, never made herself disagreeable, was never cross; and Emily, with her strong perceptions and keen intelligence, knew all her mother's excellence, and loved it the better because of her mother's weakness. She preferred her father's company, but no one could say she neglected her mother for the sake of her father.

Hitherto she had said very little to Lady Elizabeth as to her lover. She had, in the first place, told her mother, and then had received from her mother, second-hand, her father's disapproval. At that time she had only said that it was "too late." Poor Lady Elizabeth had been able to make no useful answer to this. It certainly was too late. The evil should have been avoided by refusing admittance to Cousin George both in London and at

Humblethwaite. It certainly was too late;—too late, that is, to avoid the evil altogether. The girl had been asked for her heart, and had given it. It was very much too late. But evils such as that do admit of remedy. It is not every girl that can marry the man whom she first confesses that she loves. Lady Elizabeth had some idea that her child, being nobler born and of more importance than other people's children, ought to have been allowed by fate to do so,—as there certainly is a something withdrawn from the delicate aroma of a first-class young woman by any transfer of affections;—but if it might not be so, even an Emily Hotspur must submit to a lot not uncommon among young women in general, and wait and wish till she could acknowledge to herself that her heart was susceptible of another wound. That was the mother's hope at present,—her hope, when she was positively told by Sir Harry that George Hotspur was quite out of the question as a husband for the heiress of Humblethwaite. But this would probably come the sooner if little or nothing were said of George Hotspur.

The reader need hardly be told that Emily herself regarded the matter in a very different light. She also had her ideas about the delicacy and the aroma of a maiden's love. She had confessed her love very boldly to the man who had asked for it; had made her rich present with a free hand, and had grudged nothing in the making of it. But having given it, she understood it to be fixed as the heavens that she could never give the same gift again. It was herself that she had given, and there was no retracting the offering. She had thought, and had then hoped, and had afterwards hoped more faintly, that the present had been well bestowed;—that in giving it she had disposed of herself well. Now they told her that it was not so, and that she could hardly have disposed of herself worse. She would not believe that; but, let it be as it might, the thing was done. She was his. He had a right in her which she could not withdraw from him. Was not this sort of giving acknowledged by all churches in which the words for "better or for worse" were uttered as part of the marriage vow? Here there had been as yet no church vow, and therefore her duty was still due to her father. But the sort of sacrifice,—so often a sacrifice of the good to the bad,—which the Church not only allowed but required and sanctified, could be as well conveyed by one promise as by another. What is a vow but a promise? and by what process are such vows and promises made fitting between a man and a woman? Is it not by that compelled rendering up of the heart which men call love? She had found that he was dearer to her than everything in the world besides; that to be near him was a luxury to her; that his voice was music to her; that the flame of his eyes was sunlight; that his touch was to her, as had never been the touch of any other human being. She could submit to him, she who never would submit to any one. She could delight to do his bidding, even though it were to bring him his slippers. She had confessed nothing of this, even to herself, till he had spoken to her on the bridge; but then, in a moment, she had known that it was so, and had not coyed the truth with him by a single nay. And now they told her that he was bad.

Bad as he was, he had been good enough to win her. 'Twas thus she argued with herself. Who was she that she should claim for herself the right of having a man that was not bad? That other man that had come to her, that Lord Alfred, was, she was told, good at all points; and he had not moved her in the least. His voice had possessed no music for her; and as for fetching his slippers for him,—he was to her one of those men who seem to be created just that they might be civil when wanted and then get out of the way! She had not been able for a moment to bring herself to think of regarding him as her husband. But this man, this bad man! From the moment that he had spoken to her on the bridge, she knew that she was his for ever.

It might be that she liked a bad man best. So she argued with herself again. If it were so she must put up with what misfortune her own taste might bring upon her. At any rate the thing was done, and why should any man be thrown over simply because the world called him bad? Was there to be no forgiveness for wrongs done between man and man, when the whole theory of our religion was made to depend on forgiveness from God to man? It is the duty of some one to reclaim an evident prodigal; and why should it not be her duty to reclaim this prodigal? Clearly, the very fact that she loved the prodigal would give her a potentiality that way which she would have with no other prodigal. It was at any rate her duty to try. It would at least be her duty if they would allow her to be near enough to him to make the attempt. Then she filled her mind with ideas of a long period of probation, in which every best energy of her existence should be given to this work of reclaiming the prodigal, so that at last she might put her own hand into one that should be clean enough to receive it. With such a task before her she could wait. She could watch him and give all her heart to his welfare, and never be impatient except that he might be made happy. As she thought of this, she told herself plainly that the work would not be easy, that there would be disappointment, almost heart-break, delays and sorrows; but she loved him, and it would be her duty; and then, if she could be successful, how great, how full of joy would be the triumph! Even if she were to fail and perish in failing, it would be her duty. As for giving him up because he had the misfortune to be bad, she would as soon give him up on the score of any other misfortune;—because he might lose a leg, or become deformed, or be stricken deaf by God's hand! One does not desert those one loves, because of their misfortunes! 'Twas thus she argued with herself, thinking that she could see,—whereas, poor child, she was so very blind!

"Mamma," she said, "has Papa gone up to town about Cousin George?"

"I do not know, my dear. He did not say why he was going."

"I think he has. I wish I could make him understand."

"Understand what, my dear?"

"All that I feel about it. I am sure it would save him much trouble. Nothing can ever separate me from my cousin."

"Pray don't say so, Emily."

"Nothing can. Is it not better that you and he should know the truth? Papa goes about trying to find out all the naughty things that George has ever done. There has been some mistake about a race meeting, and all manner of people are asked to give what Papa calls evidence that Cousin George was there. I do not doubt but George has been what people call dissipated."

"We do hear such dreadful stories!"

"You would not have thought anything about them if it had not been for me. He is not worse now than when he came down here last year. And he was always asked to Bruton Street."

"What do you mean by this, dear?"

"I do not mean to say that young men ought to do all these things, whatever they are,—getting into debt, and betting, and living fast. Of course it is very wrong. But when a young man has been brought up in that way, I do think he ought not to be thrown over by his nearest and dearest friends"—that last epithet was uttered with all the emphasis which Emily could give to it—"because he falls into temptation."

"I am afraid George has been worse than others, Emily."

"So much the more reason for trying to save him. If a man be in the water, you do not refuse to throw him a rope because the water is deep."

"But, dearest, your papa is thinking of you." Lady Elizabeth was not quick enough of thought to explain to her daughter that if the rope be of more value than the man, and if the chance of losing the rope be much greater than that of saving the man, then the rope is not thrown.

"And I am thinking of George," said Emily.

"But if it should appear that he had done things,—the wickedest things in the world?"

"I might break my heart in thinking of it, but I should never give him up."

"If he were a murderer?" suggested Lady Elizabeth, with horror.

The girl paused, feeling herself to be hardly pressed, and then came that look upon her brow which Lady Elizabeth understood as well as did Sir Harry. "Then I would be a murderer's wife," she said.

"Oh, Emily!"

"I must make you understand me, Mamma, and I want Papa to understand it too. No consideration on earth shall make me say that I will give him up. They may prove if they like that he was on all the racecourses in the world, and get that Mrs. Stackpoole to swear to it;—and it is ten times worse for a woman to go than it is for a man, at any rate;—but it will make no difference. If you and Papa tell me not to see him or write to him,—much less to marry him,—of course I shall obey you. But I shall not give him up a bit the more, and he must not be told that I will give him up. I am sure Papa will not wish that anything untrue should be told. George will always be to me the dearest thing in the whole world,—dearer than my own soul. I shall pray for him every night, and think of him all day long. And as to the property, Papa may be quite sure that he can never arrange it by any marriage that I shall make. No man shall ever speak to me in that way, if I can help it. I won't go where any man can speak to me. I will obey,—but it will be at the cost of my life. Of course I will obey Papa and you; but I cannot alter my heart. Why was he allowed to come here,—the head of our own family,—if he be so bad as this? Bad or good, he will always be all the world to me."

To such a daughter as this Lady Elizabeth had very little to say that might be of avail. She could quote Sir Harry, and entertain some dim distant wish that Cousin George might even yet be found to be not quite so black as he had been painted.

Chapter XV.

Cousin George Is Hard Pressed.

The very sensible and, as one would have thought, very manifest idea of buying up Cousin George originated with Mr. Boltby. "He will have his price, Sir Harry," said the lawyer. Then Sir Harry's eyes were opened, and so excellent did this mode of escape seem to him that he was ready to pay almost any price for the article. He saw it at a glance. Emily had high-flown notions, and would not yield; he feared that she would not yield, let Cousin George's delinquencies be shown to be as black as Styx. But if Cousin George could be made to give her up,—then Emily must yield; and, yielding in such manner, having received so rude a proof of her lover's unworthiness, it could not be but that her heart would be changed. Sir Harry's first idea of a price was very noble; all debts to be paid, a thousand a year for the present, and Scarrowby to be attached to the title. What price would be too high to pay for the extrication of his daughter from so grievous a misfortune? But Mr. Boltby was more calm. As to the payment of the debts,—yes, within a certain liberal limit. For the present, an income of five hundred pounds he thought would be almost as efficacious a bait as double the amount; and it would be well to tack to it the necessity of a residence abroad. It

might, perhaps, serve to get the young man out of the country for
a time. If the young man bargained on either of these headings,
the matter could be reconsidered by Mr. Boltby; as to settling
Scarrowby on the title, Mr. Boltby was clearly against it. "He
would raise every shilling he could on post-obits within twelve
months." At last the offer was made in the terms with which the
reader is already acquainted. George was sent off from the
lawyer's chambers with directions to consider the terms, and Mr.
Boltby gave his clerk some little instructions for perpetuating the
irritation on the young man which Hart and Stubber together
were able to produce. The young man should be made to
understand that hungry creditors, who had been promised their
money on certain conditions, could become very hungry indeed.

George Hotspur, blackguard and worthless as he was, did
not at first realize the fact that Sir Harry and Mr. Boltby were
endeavouring to buy him. He was asked to give up his cousin,
and he was told that if he did so a certain very generous amount
of pecuniary assistance should be given to him; but yet he did
not at the first glance perceive that one was to be the price of the
other,—that if he took the one he would meanly have sold the
other. It certainly would have been very pleasant to have all his
debts paid for him, and the offer of five hundred pounds a year
was very comfortable. Of the additional sum to be given when
Sir Harry should die, he did not think so much. It might probably
be a long time coming, and then Sir Harry would of course be
bound to do something for the title. As for living abroad,—he
might promise that, but they could not make him keep his
promise. He would not dislike to travel for six months, on
condition that he should be well provided with ready money.
There was much that was alluring in the offer, and he began to
think whether he could not get it all without actually abandoning
his cousin. But then he was to give a written pledge to that
effect, which, if given, no doubt would be shown to her. No; that
would not do. Emily was his prize; and though he did not value
her at her worth, not understanding such worth, still he had an

idea that she would be true to him. Then at last came upon him an understanding of the fact, and he perceived that a bribe had been offered to him.

For half a day he was so disgusted at the idea that his virtue was rampant within him. Sell his Emily for money? Never! His Emily,—and all her rich prospects, and that for a sum so inadequate! They little knew their man when they made a proposition so vile! That evening, at his club, he wrote a letter to Sir Harry, and the letter as soon as written was put into the club letter-box, addressed to the house in Bruton Street; in which, with much indignant eloquence, he declared that the Baronet little understood the warmth of his love, or the extent of his ambition in regard to the family. "I shall be quite ready to submit to any settlements," he said, "so long as the property is entailed upon the Baronet who shall come after myself; I need not say that I hope the happy fellow may be my own son."

But, on the next morning, on his first waking, his ideas were more vague, and a circumstance happened which tended to divert them from the current in which they had run on the preceding evening. When he was going through the sad work of dressing, he bethought himself that he could not at once force this marriage on Sir Harry—could not do so, perhaps, within a twelvemonth or more, let Emily be ever so true to him,—and that his mode of living had become so precarious as to be almost incompatible with that outward decency which would be necessary for him as Emily's suitor. He was still very indignant at the offer made to him, which was indeed bribery of which Sir Harry ought to be ashamed; but he almost regretted that his letter to Sir Harry had been sent. It had not been considered enough, and certainly should not have been written simply on after-dinner consideration. Something might have been inserted with the view of producing ready money, something which might have had a flavour of yielding, but which could not have been shown to Emily as an offer on his part to abandon her; and then he had a general feeling that his letter had been too grandiloquent,—all arising, no doubt, from a fall in courage incidental to a sick stomach.

But before he could get out of his hotel a visitor was upon him. Mr. Hart desired to see him. At this moment he would almost have preferred to see Captain Stubber. He remembered at the moment that Mr. Hart was acquainted with Mr. Walker, and that Mr. Walker would probably have sought the society of Mr. Hart after a late occurrence in which he, Cousin George, had taken part. He was going across to breakfast at his club, when he found himself almost forced to accompany Mr. Hart into a little private room at the left hand of the hall of the hotel. He wanted his breakfast badly, and was altogether out of humour. He had usually found Mr. Hart to be an enduring man, not irascible, though very pertinacious, and sometimes almost good-natured. For a moment he thought he would bully Mr. Hart, but when he looked into Mr. Hart's face, his heart misgave him.

"This is a most inconvenient time—," he had begun. But he hesitated, and Mr. Hart began his attack at once.

"Captain 'Oshspur—sir, let me tell you this von't do no longer."

"What won't do, Mr. Hart?"

"Vat von't do? You know vat von't do. Let me tell you this. You'll be at the Old Bailey very soon, if you don't do just vat you is told to do."

"Me at the Old Bailey!"

"Yes, Captain 'Oshspur,—you at the Old Bailey. In vat vay did you get those moneys from poor Mr. Valker? I know vat I says. More than three hundred pounds! It was card-sharping."

"Who says it was card-sharping?"

"I says so, Captain 'Oshspur, and so does Mr. Bullbean. Mr. Bullbean vill prove it." Mr. Bullbean was a gentleman known well to Mr. Hart, who had made one of the little party at Mr. Walker's establishment, by means of which Cousin George had gone, flush of money, down among his distinguished friends in Norfolk. "Vat did you do with poor Valker's moneys? It vas very hard upon poor Mr. Valker,—very hard."

"It was fair play, Mr. Hart."

"Gammon, Captain 'Oshspur! Vere is the moneys?"

"What business is that of yours?"

"Oh, very well. Bullbean is quite ready to go before a magistrate,—ready at once. I don't know how that vill help us with our pretty cousin with all the fortune."

"How will it help you then?"

"Look here, Captain 'Oshspur; I vill tell you vat vill help me, and vill help Captain Stubber, and vill help everybody. The young lady isn't for you at all. I know all about it, Captain 'Oshspur. Mr. Boltby is a very nice gentleman, and understands business."

"What is Mr. Boltby to me?"

"He is a great deal to me, because he vill pay me my moneys, and he vill pay Captain Stubber, and vill pay everybody. He vill pay you too, Captain 'Oshspur,—only you must pay poor Valker his moneys. I have promised Valker he shall have back his moneys, or Sir Harry shall know that too. You must just give up the young woman;—eh, Captain 'Oshspur!"

"I'm not going to be dictated to, Mr. Hart."

"When gentlemans is in debt they must be dictated to, or else be quodded. We mean to have our money from Mr. Boltby, and that at once. Here is the offer to pay it,—every shilling,— and to pay you! You must give the lady up. You must go to Mr. Boltby, and write just what he tells you. If you don't—!"

"Well, if I don't!"

"By the living God, before two weeks are over you shall be in prison. Bullbean saw it all. Now you know, Captain 'Oshspur. You don't like dictating to, don't you? If you don't do as you're dictated to, and that mighty sharp, as sure as my name is Abraham Hart, everything shall come out. Every d——d thing, Captain 'Oshspur! And now good morning, Captain

'Oshspur. You had better see Mr. Boltby to-day, Captain 'Oshspur."

How was a man so weighted to run for such stakes as those he was striving to carry off? When Mr. Hart left him he was not only sick in the stomach, but sick at heart also,—sick all over. He had gone from bad to worse; he had lost the knowledge of the flavour of vice and virtue; and yet now, when there was present to him the vanishing possibility of redeeming everything by this great marriage, it seemed to him that a life of honourable ease—such a life as Sir Harry would wish him to live if permitted to marry the girl and dwell among his friends at Humblethwaite—would be much sweeter, much more to his real taste, than the life which he had led for the last ten years. What had been his positive delights? In what moments had he actually enjoyed them? From first to last had there not been trouble and danger and vexation of spirit, and a savour of dirt about it all, which even to his palate had been nauseous? Would he not willingly reform? And yet, when the prospect of reform was brought within reach of his eyes, of a reform so pleasant in all its accompaniments, of reform amidst all the wealth of Humblethwaite, with Emily Hotspur by his side, there came these harpies down upon him rendering it all impossible. Thrice, in speaking of them to himself, he called them harpies; but it never occurred to him to think by what name Mr. Walker would have designated him.

But things around him were becoming so serious that he must do something. It might be that he would fall to the ground, losing everything. He could not understand about Bullbean. Bullbean had had his share of the plunder in regard to all that he had seen. The best part of the evening's entertainment had taken place after Mr. Bullbean had retired. No doubt, however, Mr. Bullbean might do him a damage.

He had written to Sir Harry, refusing altogether the offer made to him. Could he, after writing such a letter, at once go to the lawyer and accept the offer? And must he admit to himself, finally, that it was altogether beyond his power to win his cousin's hand? Was there no hope of that life at Humblethwaite which, when contemplated at a distance, had seemed to him to be so green and pleasant? And what would Emily think of him? In the midst of all his other miseries that also was a misery. He was able, though steeped in worthlessness, so to make for himself a double identity as to imagine and to personify a being who should really possess fine and manly aspirations with regard to a woman, and to look upon himself,—his second self,—as that being; and to perceive with how withering a contempt such a being would contemplate such another man as was in truth the real George Hotspur, whose actual sorrows and troubles had now become so unendurable.

Who would help him in his distress? The Altringhams were still in Scotland, and he knew well that, though Lady Altringham was fond of him, and though Lord Altringham liked him, there was no assistance to be had there of the kind that he needed. His dearly intimate distinguished friends in Norfolk, with whom he had been always "George," would not care if they heard that he had been crucified. It seemed to him that the world was very hard and very cruel. Who did care for him? There were two women who cared for him, who really loved him, who would make almost any sacrifice for him, who would even forget his sins, or at least forgive them. He was sure of that. Emily Hotspur loved him, but there were no means by which he could reach Emily Hotspur. She loved him, but she would not so far disobey her father and mother, or depart from her own word, as to receive even a letter from him. But the other friend who loved him,—he still could see her. He knew well the time at which he would find her at home, and some three or four hours after his interview with Mr. Hart he knocked at Mrs. Morton's door.

"Well, George," she said, "how does your wooing thrive?"

He had no preconceived plan in coming to her. He was possessed by that desire, which we all of us so often feel, to be comforted by sympathy; but he hardly knew even how to describe the want of it.

"It does not thrive at all," he said, throwing himself gloomily into an easy chair.

"That is bad news. Has the lady turned against you?"

"Oh no," said he, moodily,—"nothing of that sort."

"That would be impossible, would it not? Fathers are stern, but to such a one as you daughters are always kind. That is what you mean; eh, George?"

"I wish you would not chaff me, Lucy. I am not well, and I did not come to be chaffed."

"The chaffing is all to be on one side, is it, George? Well; I will say nothing to add to your discomforts. What is it ails you? You will drink liqueurs after dinner. That is what makes you so wretched. And I believe you drink them before dinner too."

"Hardly ever. I don't do such a thing three times in a month. It is not that; but things do trouble me so."

"I suppose Sir Harry is not well pleased."

"He is doing what he ought not to do, I must say that;— quite what I call ungentlemanlike. A lawyer should never be allowed to interfere between gentlemen. I wonder who would stand it, if an attorney were set to work to make all manner of inquiries about everything that he had ever done?"

"I could not, certainly. I should cave in at once, as the boys say."

"Other men have been as bad as I have, I suppose. He is sending about everywhere."

"Not only sending, George, but going himself. Do you know that Sir Harry did me the honour of visiting me?"

"No!"

"But he did. He sat there in that very chair, and talked to me in a manner that nobody ever did before, certainly. What a fine old man he is, and how handsome!"

"Yes; he is a good-looking old fellow."

"So like you, George."

"Is he?"

"Only you know, less,—less,—less, what shall I say?— less good-natured, perhaps."

"I know what you mean. He is not such a fool as I am."

"You're not a fool at all, George; but sometimes you are weak. He looks to be strong. Is she like him?"

"Very like him."

"Then she must be handsome."

"Handsome; I should think she is too!" said George, quite forgetting the description of his cousin which he had given some days previously to Mrs. Morton.

She smiled, but took no notice aloud of his blunder. She knew him so well that she understood it all. "Yes," she went on; "he came here and said some bitter things. He said more, perhaps, than he ought to have done."

"About me, Lucy?"

"I think that he spoke chiefly about myself. There was a little explanation, and then he behaved very well. I have no quarrel with him myself. He is a fine old gentleman; and having one only daughter, and a large fortune, I do not wonder that he should want to make inquiries before he gives her to you."

"He could do that without an attorney."

"Would you tell him the truth? The fact is, George, that you are not the sort of son-in-law that fathers like. I suppose it will be off; eh, George?" George made no immediate reply. "It is not likely that she should have the constancy to stick to it for years, and I am sure you will not. Has he offered you money?" Then George told her almost with accuracy the nature of the proposition made to him.

"It is very generous," she said.

"I don't see much of that."

"It certainly is very generous."

"What ought a fellow to do?"

"Only fancy, that you should come to me to ask me such a question!"

"I know you will tell me true."

"Do you love her?"

"Yes."

"With all your heart?"

"What is the meaning of that? I do love her."

"Better than her father's money?"

"Much better."

"Then stick to her through thick and thin. But you don't. I must not advise you in accordance with what you say, but with what I think. You will be beaten, certainly. She will never be your wife; and were you so married, you would not be happy with such people. But she will never be your wife. Take Sir Harry's offer, and write to her a letter, explaining how it is best for all that you should do so."

He paused a moment, and then he asked her one other question: "Would you write the letter for me, Lucy?"

She smiled again as she answered him: "Yes; if you make up your mind to do as Sir Harry asks you, I will write a draft of what I think you should say to her."

Chapter XVI.

Sir Harry's Return.

Sir Harry received the grandly worded and indignant letter which had been written at the club, and Cousin George hesitated as to that other letter which his friend was to dictate for him. Consequently it became necessary that Sir Harry should leave London before the matter was settled. In truth the old Baronet liked the grandly worded and indignant letter. It was almost such a letter as a Hotspur should write on such an occasion. There was an admission of pecuniary weakness which did not quite become a Hotspur, but otherwise the letter was a good letter. Before he left London he took the letter with him to Mr. Boltby, and on his way thither could not refrain from counting up all the good things which would befall him and his if only this young man might be reclaimed and recast in a mould such as should fit the heir of the Hotspurs. He had been very bad,—so bad that when Sir Harry counted up his sins they seemed to be as black as night. And then, as he thought of them, the father would declare to himself that he would not imperil his daughter by trusting her to one who had shown himself to be so evil. But again another mode of looking at it all would come upon him. The kind of vice of which George had been undoubtedly guilty was very distasteful to Sir Harry; it had been ignoble and ungentlemanlike vice. He had been a liar, and not only a gambler, but a professional gambler. He had not simply got into debt, but he had got into debt in a fashion that was fraudulent;—so at least Sir Harry thought. And yet, need it be said that this reprobate was beyond the reach of all forgiveness? Had not men before him done as bad, and yet were brought back within the pale of decent life? In this still vacillating mood of mind Sir Harry reached his lawyer's. Mr. Boltby did not vacillate at all. When he was shown the letter he merely smiled.

"I don't think it is a bad letter," said Sir Harry.

"Words mean so little, Sir Harry," said Mr. Boltby, "and come so cheap."

Sir Harry turned the letter over in his hand and frowned; he did not quite like to be told even by his confidential lawyer that he was mistaken. Unconsciously he was telling himself that after all George Hotspur had been born a gentleman, and that therefore, underlying all the young man's vileness and villany there must be a substratum of noble soil of which the lawyer perhaps knew nothing. Mr. Boltby saw that his client was doubting, and having given much trouble to the matter, and not being afraid of Sir Harry, he determined to speak his mind freely.

"Sir Harry," he said, "in this matter I must tell you what I really think."

"Certainly."

"I am sorry to have to speak ill of one bearing your name; and were not the matter urgent as it is, I should probably repress something of my opinion. As it is, I do not dare to do so. You could not in all London find a man less fit to be the husband of Miss Hotspur than her cousin."

"He is a gentleman—by birth," said Sir Harry.

"He is an unprincipled blackguard by education, and the more blackguard because of his birth; there is nothing too bad for him to do, and very little so bad but what he has done it. He is a gambler, a swindler, and, as I believe, a forger and a card-sharper. He has lived upon the wages of the woman he has professed to love. He has shown himself to be utterly spiritless, abominable, and vile. If my clerk in the next room were to slap his face, I do not believe that he would resent it." Sir Harry frowned, and moved his feet rapidly on the floor. "In my thorough respect and regard for you, Sir Harry," continued Mr. Boltby, "I have undertaken a work which I would not have done for above two or three other men in the world beside yourself. I am bound to tell you the result, which is this,—that I would sooner give my own girl to the sweeper at the crossing than to George Hotspur."

Sir Harry's brow was very black. Perhaps he had not quite known his lawyer. Perhaps it was that he had less power of endurance than he had himself thought in regard to the mention of his own family affairs. "Of course," he said, "I am greatly indebted to you, Mr. Boltby, for the trouble you have taken."

"I only hope it may be of service to you."

"It has been of service. What may be the result in regard to this unfortunate young man I cannot yet say. He has refused our offer,—I must say as I think—honourably."

"It means nothing."

"How nothing, Mr. Boltby?"

"No man accepts such a bargain at first. He is playing his hand against yours, Sir Harry, and he knows that he has got a very good card in his own. It was not to be supposed that he would give in at once. In besieging a town the surest way is to starve the garrison. Wait a while and he will give in. When a town has within its walls such vultures as will now settle upon him, it cannot stand out very long. I shall hear more of him before many days are over."

"You think, then, that I may return to Humblethwaite."

"Certainly, Sir Harry; but I hope, Sir Harry, that you will return with the settled conviction on your mind that this young man must not on any consideration be allowed to enter your family."

The lawyer meant well, but he overdid his work. Sir Harry got up and shook hands with him and thanked him, but left the room with some sense of offence. He had come to Mr. Boltby for information, and he had received it. But he was not quite sure that he had intended that Mr. Boltby should advise him touching his management of his own daughter. Mr. Boltby, he thought, had gone a little beyond his tether. Sir Harry acknowledged to himself that he had learned a great deal about his cousin, and it was for him to judge after that whether he would receive his cousin at Humblethwaite. Mr. Boltby should not have spoken about the crossing-sweeper. And then Sir Harry was not quite sure that he liked that idea of setting vultures upon a man; and Sir Harry remembered something of his old lore as a hunting man. It is astonishing what blood will do in bringing a horse through mud at the end of a long day. Mr. Boltby probably did not understand how much, at the very last, might be expected from breeding. When Sir Harry left Mr. Boltby's chambers he was almost better-minded towards Cousin George than he had been when he entered them; and in this frame of mind, both for and against the young man, he returned to Humblethwaite. It must not be supposed, however, that as the result of the whole he was prepared to yield. He knew, beyond all doubt, that his cousin was thoroughly a bad subject,—a worthless and, as he believed, an irredeemable scamp; but yet he thought of what might happen if he were to yield!

Things were very sombre when he reached Humblethwaite. Of course his wife could not refrain from questions. "It is very bad," he said,—"as bad as can be."

"He has gambled?"

"Gambled! If that were all! You had better not ask about it; he is a disgrace to the family."

"Then there can be no hope for Emily?"

"No hope! Why should there not be hope? All her life need not depend on her fancy for a man of whom after all she has not seen so very much. She must get over it. Other girls have had to do the same."

"She is not like other girls, Harry."

"How not like them?"

"I think she is more persistent; she has set her heart upon loving this young man, and she will love him."

"Then she must."

"She will break her heart," said Lady Elizabeth.

"She will break mine, I know," said Sir Harry.

When he met his daughter he had embraced her, and she had kissed him and asked after his welfare; but he felt at once that she was different from what she used to be,—different, not only as regarded herself, but different also in her manner. There came upon him a sad, ponderous conviction that the sunlight had gone out from their joint lives, that all pleasant things were over for both of them, and that, as for him, it would be well for him that he should die. He could not be happy if there were discord between him and his child,—and there must be discord. The man had been invited with a price to take himself off, and had not been sufficiently ignoble to accept the offer. How could he avoid the discord, and bring back the warmth of the sun into his house? Then he remembered those terribly forcible epithets which Mr. Boltby had spoken. "He is an unprincipled blackguard; and the worse blackguard because of his birth." The words had made Sir Harry angry, but he believed them to be true. If there were to be any yielding, he would not yield as yet; but that living in his house without sunshine was very grievous to him. "She will kill me," he said to himself, "if she goes on like this."

And yet it was hard to say of what it was that he complained. Days went by and his daughter said nothing and did nothing of which he could complain. It was simply this,—that the sunshine was no longer bright within his halls. Days went by, and George Hotspur's name had never been spoken by Emily in the hearing of her father or mother. Such duties as there were for her to do were done. The active duties of a girl in her position are very few. It was her custom of a morning to spread butter on a bit of toast for her father to eat. This she still did, and brought it to him as was her wont; but she did not bring it with her old manner. It was a thing still done,—simply because not to do it would be an omission to be remarked. "Never mind it," said her father the fourth or fifth morning after his return, "I'd sooner do it for myself." She did not say a word, but on the next morning the little ceremony, which had once been so full of pleasant affection, was discontinued. She had certain hours of reading, and these were prolonged rather than abandoned. But both her father and mother perceived that her books were changed; her Italian was given up, and she took to works of religion,— sermons, treatises, and long commentaries.

"It will kill me," said Sir Harry to his wife.

"I am afraid it will kill her," said Lady Elizabeth. "Do you see how her colour has gone, and she eats so little!"

"She walks every day."

"Yes; and comes in so tired. And she goes to church every Wednesday and Friday at Hesket. I'm sure she is not fit for it such weather as this."

"She has the carriage?"

"No, she walks."

Then Sir Harry gave orders that his daughter should always have the carriage on Wednesdays and Fridays. But Emily, when her mother told her this, insisted that she would sooner walk.

But what did the carriage or no carriage on Wednesday signify? The trouble was deeper than that. It was so deep that both father and mother felt that something must be done, or the trouble would become too heavy for their backs. Ten days passed and nothing was heard either from Mr. Boltby or from Cousin George. Sir Harry hardly knew what it was then he expected to hear; but it seemed that he did expect something. He was nervous at the hour of post, and was aware himself that he was existing on from day to day with the idea of soon doing some special thing,—he knew not what,—but something that might put an end to the frightful condition of estrangement between him and his child in which he was now living. It told even upon his duty among his tenants. It told upon his farm. It told upon almost every workman in the parish. He had no heart for doing anything. It did not seem certain to him that he could continue to live in his own house. He could not bring himself to order that this wood should be cut, or that those projected cottages should be built. Everything was at a standstill; and it was clear to him that Emily knew that all this had come from her rash love for her cousin George. She never now came and stood at his elbow in his own room, or leaned upon his shoulder; she never now asked him questions, or brought him out from his papers to decide questions in the garden,—or rather to allow himself to be ruled by her decisions. There were greetings between them morning and evening, and questions were asked and answered formally; but there was no conversation. "What have I done that I should be punished in this way?" said Sir Harry to himself.

If he was prompt to think himself hardly used, so also was his daughter. In considering the matter in her own mind she had found it to be her duty to obey her father in her outward conduct, founding her convictions in this matter upon precedent and upon the general convictions of the world. In the matter of bestowing herself upon a suitor, a girl is held to be subject to her parents. So much she knew, or believed that she knew; and therefore she would obey. She had read and heard of girls who would correspond with their lovers clandestinely, would run away with their lovers, would marry their lovers as it were behind their fathers' backs. No act of this kind would she do. She had something within her which would make it dreadful to her ever to have to admit that she had been personally wrong,— some mixture of pride and principle, which was strong enough to keep her steadfast in her promised obedience. She would do nothing that could be thrown in her teeth; nothing that could be called unfeminine, indelicate, or undutiful. But she had high ideas of what was due to herself, and conceived that she would be wronged by her father, should her father take advantage of her sense of duty to crush her heart. She had her own rights and her own privileges, with which grievous and cruel interference would be made, should her father, because he was her father, rob her of the only thing which was sweet to her taste or desirable in her esteem. Because she was his heiress he had no right to make her his slave. But even should he do so, she had in her own hands a certain security. The bondage of a slave no doubt he might allot to her, but not the task-work. Because she would cling to her duty and keep the promise which she had made to him, it would be in his power to prevent the marriage upon which she had set her heart; but it was not within his power, or within his privilege as a father, to force upon her any other marriage. She would never help him with her hand in that adjustment of his property of which he thought so much unless he would help her in her love. And in the meantime sunshine should be banished from the house, such sunshine as had shone round her head. She did not so esteem herself as to suppose that, because she was sad, therefore her father and mother would be wretched; but she did feel herself bound to contribute to the house in general all the wretchedness which might come from her own want of sunlight. She suffered under a terrible feeling of ill-usage. Why was she, because she was a girl and an heiress, to be debarred from her own happiness? If she were willing to risk herself, why should others interfere? And if the life and conduct of her cousin were in truth so bad as they were represented,— which she did not in the least believe,—why had he been allowed to come within her reach? It was not only that he was young, clever, handsome, and in every way attractive, but that, in addition to all this, he was a Hotspur, and would some day be the head of the Hotspurs. Her father had known well enough that her family pride was equal to his own. Was it not natural that, when a man so endowed had come in her way, she should learn to love him? And when she had loved him, was it not right that she should cling to her love?

Her father would fain treat her like a beast of burden kept in the stables for a purpose; or like a dog whose obedience and affections might be transferred from one master to another for a price. She would obey her father; but her father should be made to understand that hers was not the nature of a beast of burden or of a dog. She was a Hotspur as thoroughly as was he. And then they brought men there to her, selected suitors, whom she despised. What did they think of her when imagining that she would take a husband not of her own choosing? What must be their idea of love, and of marriage duty, and of that close intercourse of man and wife? To her feeling a woman should not marry at all unless she could so love a man as to acknowledge to herself that she was imperatively required to sacrifice all that belonged to her for his welfare and good. Such was her love for George Hotspur,—let him be what he might. They told her that he was bad and that he would drag her into the mud. She was willing to be dragged into the mud; or, at any rate, to make her own struggle during the dragging, as to whether he should drag her in, or she should drag him out.

And then they brought men to her—walking-sticks,— Lord Alfred and young Mr. Thoresby, and insulted her by supposing of her that she would marry a man simply because he was brought there as a fitting husband. She would be dutiful and obedient as a daughter, according to her idea of duty and of principle; but she would let them know that she had an identity of her own, and that she was not to be moulded like a piece of clay.

No doubt she was hard upon her father. No doubt she was in very truth disobedient and disrespectful. It was not that she should have married any Lord Alfred that was brought to her, but that she should have struggled to accommodate her spirit to her father's spirit. But she was a Hotspur; and though she could be generous, she could not yield. And then the hold of a child upon the father is so much stronger than that of the father on the child! Our eyes are set in our face, and are always turned forward. The glances that we cast back are but occasional.

And so the sunshine was banished from the house of Humblethwaite, and the days were as black as the night.

Chapter XVII.

"Let Us Try."

Things went on thus at Humblethwaite for three weeks, and Sir Harry began to feel that he could endure it no longer. He had expected to have heard again from Mr. Boltby, but no letter had come. Mr. Boltby had suggested to him something of starving out the town, and he had expected to be informed before this whether the town were starved out or not. He had received an indignant and grandiloquent letter from his cousin, of which as yet he had taken no notice. He had taken no notice of the letter, although it had been written to decline a proposal of very great moment made by himself. He felt that in these circumstances Mr. Boltby ought to have written to him. He ought to have been told what was being done. And yet he had left Mr. Boltby with a feeling which made it distasteful to him to ask further questions from the lawyer on the subject. Altogether his position was one as disagreeable and painful as it well could be.

But at last, in regard to his own private life with his daughter, he could bear it no longer. The tenderness of his heart was too much for his pride, and he broke down in his resolution to be stern and silent with her till all this should have passed by

them. She was so much more to him than he was to her! She was
his all in all;—whereas Cousin George was hers. He was the
happier at any rate in this, that he would never be forced to
despise where he loved.

"Emily," he said to her at last, "why is it that you are so
changed to me?"

"Papa!"

"Are you not changed? Do you not know that everything
about the house is changed?"

"Yes, Papa."

"And why is it so? I do not keep away from you. You
used to come to me every day. You never come near me now."

She hesitated for a moment with her eyes turned to the
ground, and then as she answered him she looked him full in the
face. "It is because I am always thinking of my cousin George."

"But why should that keep us apart, Emily? I wish that it
were not so; but why should that keep us apart?"

"Because you are thinking of him too, and think so
differently! You hate him; but I love him."

"I do not hate him. It is not that I hate him. I hate his
vices."

"So do I."

"I know that he is not a fit man for you to marry. I have
not been able to tell you the things that I know of him."

"I do not wish to be told."

"But you might believe me when I assure you that they
are of a nature to make you change your feelings towards him.
At this very moment he is attached to—to—another person."

Emily Hotspur blushed up to her brows, and her cheeks
and forehead were suffused with blood; but her mouth was set as
firm as a rock, and then came that curl over her eye which her
father had so dearly loved when she was a child, but which was
now held by him to be so dangerous. She was not going to be
talked out of her love in that way. Of course there had been
things,—were things of which she knew nothing and desired to

know nothing. Though she herself was as pure as the driven snow, she did not require to be told that there were impurities in the world. If it was meant to be insinuated that he was untrue to her, she simply disbelieved it. But what if he were? His untruth would not justify hers. And untruth was impossible to her. She loved him, and had told him so. Let him be ever so false, it was for her to bring him back to truth or to spend herself in the endeavour. Her father did not understand her at all when he talked to her after this fashion. But she said nothing. Her father was alluding to a matter on which she could say nothing.

"If I could explain to you the way in which he has raised money for his daily needs, you would feel that he had degraded himself beneath your notice."

"He cannot degrade himself beneath my notice;—not now. It is too late."

"But, Emily,—do you mean to say then that, let you set your affections where you might,—however wrongly, on however base a subject,—your mamma and I ought to yield to them, merely because they are so set?"

"He is your heir, Papa."

"No; you are my heir. But I will not argue upon that. Grant that he were my heir; even though every acre that is mine must go to feed his wickedness the very moment that I die, would that be a reason for giving my child to him also? Do you think that you are no more to me than the acres, or the house, or the empty title? They are all nothing to my love for you."

"Papa!"

"I do not think that you have known it. Nay, darling, I have hardly known it myself. All other anxieties have ceased with me now that I have come to know what it really is to be anxious for you. Do you think that I would not abandon any consideration as to wealth or family for your happiness? It has come to that with me, Emily, that they are nothing to me now;— nothing. You are everything."

"Dear Papa!" And now once again she leant upon his shoulder.

"When I tell you of the young man's life, you will not listen to me. You regard it simply as groundless opposition."

"No, Papa; not groundless,—only useless."

"But am I not bound to see that my girl be not united to a man who would disgrace her, misuse her, drag her into the dirt,"—that idea of dragging George out was strong in Emily's mind as she listened to this,—"make her wretched and contemptible, and degrade her? Surely this is a father's duty; and my child should not turn from me, and almost refuse to speak to me, because I do it as best I can!"

"I do not turn from you, Papa."

"Has my darling been to me as she used to be?"

"Look here, Papa; you know what it is I have promised you."

"I do, dearest."

"I will keep my promise. I will never marry him till you consent. Even though I were to see him every day for ten years, I would not do so when I had given my word."

"I am sure of it, Emily."

"But let us try, you and I and Mamma together. If you will do that; oh, I will be so good to you! Let us see if we cannot make him good. I will never ask to marry him till you yourself are satisfied that he has reformed." She looked into his face imploringly, and she saw that he was vacillating. And yet he was a strong man, not given in ordinary things to much doubt. "Papa, let us understand each other and be friends. If we do not trust each other, who can trust any one?"

"I do trust you."

"I shall never care for any one else."

"Do not say that, my child. You are too young to know your own heart. These are wounds which time will cure. Others have suffered as you are suffering, and yet have become happy wives and mothers."

"Papa, I shall never change. I think I love him more because he is—so weak. Like a poor child that is a cripple, he wants more love than those who are strong. I shall never change. And look here, Papa; I know it is my duty to obey you by not marrying without your consent. But it can never be my duty to marry any one because you or Mamma ask me. You will agree to that, Papa?"

"I should never think of pressing any one on you."

"That is what I mean. And so we do understand each other. Nothing can teach me not to think of him, and to love him, and to pray for him. As long as I live I shall do so. Nothing you can find out about him will alter me in that. Pray, pray do not go on finding out bad things. Find out something good, and then you will begin to love him."

"But if there is nothing good?" Sir Harry, as he said this, remembered the indignant refusal of his offer which was at that moment in his pocket, and confessed to himself that he had no right to say that nothing good could be found in Cousin George.

"Do not say that, Papa. How can you say that of any one? Remember, he has our name, and he must some day be at the head of our family."

"It will not be long, first," said Sir Harry, mournfully.

"Many, many, many years, I hope. For his sake as well as ours, I pray that it may be so. But still it is natural to suppose that the day will come."

"Of course it will come."

"Must it not be right, then, to make him fit for it when it comes? It can't be your great duty to think of him, as it is mine; but still it must be a duty to you too. I will not excuse his life, Papa; but have there not been temptations,—such great temptations? And then, other men are excused for doing what he has done. Let us try together, Papa. Say that you will try."

It was clear to Sir Harry through it all that she knew nothing as yet of the nature of the man's offences. When she spoke of temptation not resisted, she was still thinking of commonplace extravagance, of the ordinary pleasures of fast young men, of racecourses, and betting, perhaps, and of tailors' bills. That lie which he had told about Goodwood she had, as it were, thrown behind her, so that she should not be forced to look at it. But Sir Harry knew him to be steeped in dirty lies up to the hip, one who cheated tradesmen on system, a gambler who looked out for victims, a creature so mean that he could take a woman's money! Mr. Boltby had called him a swindler, a card-sharper, and a cur; and Sir Harry, though he was inclined at the present moment to be angry with Mr. Boltby, had never known the lawyer to be wrong. And this was the man for whom his daughter was pleading with all the young enthusiasm of her nature,—was pleading, not as for a cousin, but in order that he might at last be welcomed to that house as her lover, her husband, the one human being chosen out from all the world to be the recipient of the good things of which she had the bestowal! The man was so foul in the estimation of Sir Harry that it was a stain to be in his presence; and this was the man whom he as a father was implored to help to save, in order that at some future time his daughter might become the reprobate's wife!

"Papa, say that you will help me," repeated Emily, clinging to him, and looking up into his face.

He could not say that he would help her, and yet he longed to say some word that might comfort her. "You have been greatly shaken by all this, dearest."

"Shaken! Yes, in one sense I have been shaken. I don't know quite what you mean. I shall never be shaken in the other way."

"You have been distressed."

"Yes; distressed."

"And, indeed, so have we all," he continued. "I think it will be best to leave this for a while."

"For how long, Papa?"

"We need not quite fix that. I was thinking of going to Naples for the winter." He was silent, waiting for her approbation, but she expressed none. "It is not long since you said how much you would like to spend a winter in Naples."

She still paused, but it was but for a moment. "At that time, Papa, I was not engaged." Did she mean to tell him, that because of this fatal promise which she had made, she never meant to stir from her home till she should be allowed to go with that wretch as her husband; that because of this promise, which could never be fulfilled, everything should come to an end with her? "Papa," she said, "that would not be the way to try to save him, to go away and leave him among those who prey upon him;—unless, indeed, he might go too!"

"What! with us?"

"With you and Mamma. Why not? You know what I have promised. You can trust me."

"It is a thing absolutely not to be thought of," he said; and then he left her. What was he to do? He could take her abroad, no doubt, but were he to do so in her present humour, she would, of course, relapse into that cold, silent, unloving, undutiful obedience which had been so distressing to him. She had made a great request to him, and he had not absolutely refused it. But the more he thought of it the more distasteful did it become to him. You cannot touch pitch and not be defiled. And the stain of this pitch was so very black! He could pay money, if that would soothe her. He could pay money, even if the man should not accept the offer made to him, should she demand it of him. And if the man would reform himself, and come out through the fire really purified, might it not be possible that at some long future time Emily should become his wife? Or, if some sort of half promise such as this were made to Emily, would not that soften her for the time, and induce her to go abroad with a spirit capable of satisfaction, if not of pleasure? If this could be brought about, then time might do the rest. It would have been a delight to him to see his daughter married early, even though his own home might have been made desolate; but now he would be content if he thought he could look forward to some future settlement in life that might become her rank and fortune.

Emily, when her father left her, was aware that she had received no reply to her request, which she was entitled to regard as encouraging; but she thought that she had broken the ice, and that her father would by degrees become accustomed to her plan. If she could only get him to say that he would watch over the unhappy one, she herself would not be unhappy. It was not to be expected that she should be allowed to give her own aid at first to the work, but she had her scheme. His debts must be paid, and an income provided for him. And duties, too, must be given to him. Why should he not live at Scarrowby, and manage the property there? And then, at length, he would be welcomed to Humblethwaite, when her own work might begin. Neither for him nor for her must there be any living again in London until this task should have been completed. That any trouble could be too great, any outlay of money too vast for so divine a purpose, did not occur to her. Was not this man the heir to her father's title; and was he not the owner of her own heart? Then she knelt down and prayed that the Almighty Father would accomplish this good work for her;—and yet, not for her, but for him; not that she might be happy in her love, but that he might be as a brand saved from the burning, not only hereafter, but here also, in the sight of men. Alas, dearest, no; not so could it be done! Not at thy instance, though thy prayers be as pure as the songs of angels;—but certainly at his, if only he could be taught to know that the treasure so desirable in thy sight, so inestimable to thee, were a boon worthy of his acceptance.

Chapter XVIII.

Good Advice.

Two or three days after the little request made by Cousin George to Mrs. Morton, the Altringhams came suddenly to town. George received a note from Lady Altringham addressed to him at his club.

> We are going through to the Draytons in Hampshire. It is a new freak. Four or five horses are to be sold, and Gustavus thinks of buying the lot. If you are in town, come to us. You must not think that we are slack about you because Gustavus would have nothing to do with the money. He will be at home to-morrow till eleven. I shall not go out till two. We leave on Thursday.
>
> —Yours,
>
> A. A.

This letter he received on the Wednesday. Up to that hour he had done nothing since his interview with Mr. Hart; nor during those few days did he hear from that gentleman, or from Captain Stubber, or from Mr. Boltby. He had written to Sir Harry refusing Sir Harry's generous offer, and subsequently to that had made up his mind to accept it,—and had asked, as the reader knows, for Mrs. Morton's assistance. But the making up of George Hotspur's mind was nothing. It was unmade again that day after dinner, as he thought of all the glories of Humblethwaite and Scarrowby combined. Any one knowing him would have been sure that he would do nothing till he should be further driven. Now there had come upon the scene in London one who could drive him.

He went to the Earl's house just at eleven, not wishing to seem to avoid the Earl, but still desirous of seeing as little of his friend on that occasion as possible. He found Lord Altringham standing in his wife's morning-room. "How are you, old fellow? How do things go with the heiress?" He was in excellent humour, and said nothing about the refused request. "I must be off. You do what my Lady advises; you may be sure that she knows a deal more about it than you or I." Then he went, wishing George success in his usual friendly, genial way, which, as George knew, meant very little.

With Lady Altringham the case was different. She was in earnest about it. It was to her a matter of real moment that this great heiress should marry one of her own set, and a man who wanted money so badly as did poor George. And she liked work of that kind. George's matrimonial prospects were more interesting to her than her husband's stables. She was very soon in the thick of it all, asking questions, and finding out how the land lay. She knew that George would lie; but that was to be expected from a man in his position. She knew also that she could with fair accuracy extract the truth from his lies.

"Pay all your debts, and give you five hundred pounds a year for his life."

"The lawyer has offered that," said George, sadly.

"Then you may be sure," continued Lady Altringham, "that the young lady is in earnest. You have not accepted it?"

"Oh dear, no. I wrote to Sir Harry quite angrily. I told him I wanted my cousin's hand."

"And what next?"

"I have heard nothing further from anybody."

Lady Altringham sat and thought. "Are these people in London bothering you?" George explained that he had been bothered a good deal, but not for the last four or five days. "Can they put you in prison, or anything of that kind?"

George was not quite sure whether they might or might not have some such power. He had a dreadful weight on his mind of which he could say nothing to Lady Altringham. Even she would be repelled from him were she to know of that evening's work between him and Messrs. Walker and Bullbean. He said at last that he did not think they could arrest him, but that he was not quite sure.

"You must do something to let her know that you are as much in earnest as she is."

"Exactly."

"It is no use writing, because she wouldn't get your letters."

"She wouldn't have a chance."

"And if I understand her she would not do anything secretly."

"I am afraid not," said George.

"You will live, perhaps, to be glad that it is so. When girls come out to meet their lovers clandestinely before marriage, they get so fond of the excitement that they sometimes go on doing it afterwards."

"She is as,—as—as sure to go the right side of the post as any girl in the world."

"No doubt. So much the better for you. When those girls do catch the disease, they always have it very badly. They mean only to have one affair, and naturally want to make the most of it. Well, now what I would do is this. Run down to Humblethwaite."

"To Humblethwaite!"

"Yes. I don't suppose you are going to be afraid of anybody. Knock at the door, and send your card to Sir Harry.

Drive into the stable-yard, so that everybody about the place may know that you are there, and then ask to see the Baronet."

"He wouldn't see me."

"Then ask to see Lady Elizabeth."

"She wouldn't be allowed to see me."

"Then leave a letter, and say that you'll wait for an answer. Write to Miss Hotspur whatever you like to say in the way of a love-letter, and put it under cover to Sir Harry—open."

"She'll never get it."

"I don't suppose she will. Not but what she may—only that isn't the first object. But this will come of it. She'll know that you've been there. That can't be kept from her. You may be sure that she was very firm in sticking to you when he offered to pay all that money to get rid of you. She'll remain firm if she's made to know that you are the same. Don't let her love die out for want of notice."

"I won't."

"If they take her abroad, go after them. Stick to it, and you'll wear them out if she helps you. And if she knows that you are sticking to it, she'll do the same for honour. When she begins to be a little pale, and to walk out at nights, and to cough in the morning, they'll be tired out and send for Dr. George Hotspur. That's the way it will go if you play your game well."

Cousin George was lost in admiration at the wisdom and generalship of this great counsellor, and promised implicit obedience. The Countess went on to explain that it might be expedient to postpone this movement for a week or two. "You should leave just a little interval, because you cannot always be doing something. For some days after his return her father won't cease to abuse you, which will keep you well in her mind. When those men begin to attack you again, so as to make London too hot, then run down to Humblethwaite. Don't hide your light under a bushel. Let the people down there know all about it."

George Hotspur swore eternal gratitude and implicit obedience, and went back to his club.

Mr. Hart and Captain Stubber did not give him much rest. From Mr. Boltby he received no further communication. For the present Mr. Boltby thought it well to leave him in the hands of Mr. Hart and Captain Stubber. Mr. Boltby, indeed, did not as yet know of Mr. Bullbean's story, although certain hints had reached him which had, as he thought, justified him in adding the title of card-sharper to those other titles with which he had decorated his client's cousin's name. Had he known the entire Walker story, he would probably have thought that Cousin George might have been bought at a considerably cheaper price than that fixed in the Baronet's offer, which was still in force. But then Mr. Hart had his little doubts also and his difficulties. He, too, could perceive that were he to make this last little work of Captain Hotspur's common property in the market, it might so far sink Captain Hotspur's condition and value in the world that nobody would think it worth his while to pay Captain Hotspur's debts. At present there was a proposition from an old gentleman, possessed of enormous wealth, to "pay all Captain Hotspur's debts." Three months ago, Mr. Hart would willingly have sold every scrap of the Captain's paper in his possession for the half of the sum inscribed on it. The whole sum was now promised, and would undoubtedly be paid if the Captain could be worked upon to do as Mr. Boltby desired. But if the gentlemen employed on this delicate business were to blow upon the Captain too severely, Mr. Boltby would have no such absolute necessity to purchase the Captain. The Captain would sink to zero, and not need purchasing. Mr. Walker must have back his money,—or so much of it as Mr. Hart might permit him to take. That probably might be managed; and the Captain must be thoroughly frightened, and must be made to write the letter which Mr. Boltby desired. Mr. Hart understood his work very well;—so, it is hoped, does the reader.

Captain Stubber was in these days a thorn in our hero's side; but Mr. Hart was a scourge of scorpions. Mr. Hart never ceased to talk of Mr. Walker, and of the determination of Walker and Bullbean to go before a magistrate if restitution were not made. Cousin George of course denied the foul play, but admitted that he would repay the money if he had it. There should be no difficulty about the money, Mr. Hart assured him, if he would only write that letter to Mr. Boltby. In fact, if he would write that letter to Mr. Boltby, he should be made "shquare all round." So Mr. Hart was pleased to express himself. But if this were not done, and done at once, Mr. Hart swore by his God that Captain "'Oshspur" should be sold up, root and branch, without another day's mercy. The choice was between five hundred pounds a year in any of the capitals of Europe, and that without a debt,—or penal servitude. That was the pleasant form in which Mr. Hart put the matter to his young friend.

Cousin George drank a good deal of curaçoa, and doubted between Lady Altringham and Mr. Hart. He knew that he had not told everything to the Countess. Excellent as was her scheme, perfect as was her wisdom, her advice was so far more dangerous than the Jew's, that it was given somewhat in the dark. The Jew knew pretty well everything. The Jew was interested, of course, and therefore his advice must also be regarded with suspicion. At last, when Mr. Hart and Captain Stubber between them had made London too hot to hold him, he started for Humblethwaite,—not without leaving a note for "dear Mr. Hart," in which he explained to that gentleman that he was going to Westmoreland suddenly, with a purpose that would, he trusted, very speedily enable him to pay every shilling that he owed.

"Yesh," said Mr. Hart, "and if he ain't quick he shall come back with a 'andcuff on."

Captain Hotspur could not very well escape Mr. Hart. He started by the night-train for Penrith, and before doing so prepared a short letter for Miss Hotspur, which, as instructed, he put open under an envelope addressed to the Baronet. There should be nothing clandestine, nothing dishonourable. Oh dear, no! He quite taught himself to believe that he would have hated anything dishonourable or clandestine. His letter was as follows:—

> DEAREST EMILY,—
>
> After what has passed between us, I cannot bear not to attempt to see you or to write to you. So I shall go down and take this letter with me. Of course I shall not take any steps of which Sir Harry might disapprove. I wrote to him two or three weeks ago, telling him what I proposed, and I thought that he would have answered me. As I have not heard from him I shall take this with me to Humblethwaite, and shall hope, though I do not know whether I may dare to expect, to see the girl I love better than all the world.
>
> —Always your own,
>
> GEORGE HOTSPUR.

Even this was not composed by himself, for Cousin George, though he could often talk well,—or at least sufficiently well for the purposes which he had on hand,—was not good with his pen on such an occasion as this. Lady Altringham had sent him by post a rough copy of what he had better say, and he had copied her ladyship's words verbatim. There is no matter of doubt at all but that on all such subjects an average woman can write a better letter than an average man; and Cousin George was therefore right to obtain assistance from his female friends.

He slept at Penrith till nearly noon, then breakfasted and started with post-horses for Humblethwaite. He felt that everybody knew what he was about, and was almost ashamed of being seen. Nevertheless he obeyed his instructions. He had himself driven up through the lodges and across the park into the large stable-yard of the Hall. Lady Altringham had quite understood that more people must see and hear him in this way than if he merely rang at the front door and were from thence dismissed. The grooms and the coachman saw him, as did also three or four of the maids who were in the habit of watching to see that the grooms and coachman did their work. He had brought with him a travelling-bag,—not expecting to be asked to stay and dine, but thinking it well to be prepared. This, however, he left in the fly as he walked round to the hall-door. The footman was already there when he appeared, as word had gone through the house that Mr. George had arrived. Was Sir Harry at home? Yes, Sir Harry was at home;—and then George found himself in a small parlour, or book-room, or subsidiary library, which he had very rarely known to be used. But there was a fire in the room, and he stood before it, twiddling his hat.

In a quarter of an hour the door was opened, and the servant came in with a tray and wine and sandwiches. George felt it to be an inappropriate welcome; but still, after a fashion, it was a welcome.

"Is Sir Harry in the house?" he asked.

"Yes, Mr. Hotspur."

"Does he know that I am here?"

"Yes, Mr. Hotspur, I think he does."

Then it occurred to Cousin George that perhaps he might bribe the servant; and he put his hand into his pocket. But before he had communicated the two half-crowns, it struck him that there was no possible request which he could make to the man in reference to which a bribe would be serviceable.

"Just ask them to look to the horses," he said; "I don't know whether they were taken out."

"The horses is feeding, Mr. Hotspur," said the man.

Every word the man spoke was gravely spoken, and George understood perfectly that he was held to have done a very wicked thing in coming to Humblethwaite. Nevertheless, there was a decanter full of sherry, which, as far as it went, was an emblem of kindness. Nobody should say that he was unwilling to accept kindness at his cousin's hands, and he helped himself liberally. Before he was interrupted again he had filled his glass four times.

But in truth it needed something to support him. For a whole hour after the servant's disappearance he was left alone.

There were books in the room,—hundreds of them; but in such circumstances who could read? Certainly not Cousin George, to whom books at no time gave much comfort. Twice and thrice he stepped towards the bell, intending to ring it, and ask again for Sir Harry; but twice and thrice he paused. In his position he was bound not to give offence to Sir Harry. At last the door was opened, and with silent step, and grave demeanour, and solemn countenance, Lady Elizabeth walked into the room. "We are very sorry that you should have been kept so long waiting, Captain Hotspur," she said.

Chapter XIX.

The New Smithy.

Sir Harry was sitting alone in the library when the tidings were brought to him that George Hotspur had reached Humblethwaite with a pair of post-horses from Penrith. The old butler, Cloudesdale, brought him the news, and Cloudesdale whispered it into his ears with solemn sorrow. Cloudesdale was well aware that Cousin George was no credit to the house of Humblethwaite. And much about the same time the information was brought to Lady Elizabeth by her housekeeper, and to Emily by her own maid. It was by Cloudesdale's orders that George was shown into the small room near the hall; and he told Sir Harry what he had done in a funereal whisper. Lady Altringham had been quite right in her method of ensuring the general delivery of the information about the house.

Emily flew at once to her mother. "George is here," she said. Mrs. Quick, the housekeeper, was at that moment leaving the room.

"So Quick tells me. What can have brought him, my dear?"

"Why should he not come, Mamma?"

"Because your papa will not make him welcome to the house. Oh, dear,—he knows that. What are we to do?" In a few minutes Mrs. Quick came back again. Sir Harry would be much obliged if her ladyship would go to him. Then it was that the sandwiches and sherry were ordered. It was a compromise on the part of Lady Elizabeth between Emily's prayer that some welcome might be shown, and Sir Harry's presumed determination that the banished man should continue to be regarded as banished. "Take him some kind of refreshment, Quick;—a glass of wine or something, you know." Then Mrs. Quick had cut the sandwiches with her own hand, and Cloudesdale had given the sherry. "He ain't eaten much, but he's made it up with the wine," said Cloudesdale, when the tray was brought back again.

Lady Elizabeth went down to her husband, and there was a consultation. Sir Harry was quite clear that he would not now, on this day, admit Cousin George as a guest into his house; nor would he see him. To that conclusion he came after his wife had been with him some time. He would not see him, there, at Humblethwaite. If George had anything to say that could not be said in a letter, a meeting might be arranged elsewhere. Sir Harry confessed, however, that he could not see that good results could come from any meeting whatsoever. "The truth is, that I don't want to have anything more to do with him," said Sir Harry. That was all very well, but as Emily's wants in this respect were at variance with her father's, there was a difficulty. Lady Elizabeth pleaded that some kind of civility, at least some mitigation of opposition, should be shown, for Emily's sake. At last she was commissioned to go to Cousin George, to send him away from the house, and, if necessary, to make an appointment between him and Sir Harry at the Crown, at Penrith, for the morrow. Nothing on earth should induce Sir Harry to see his cousin anywhere on his own premises. As for any meeting between Cousin George and Emily, that was, of course, out of the question,—and he must go from Humblethwaite. Such were the instructions with which Lady Elizabeth descended to the little room.

Cousin George came forward with the pleasantest smile to take Lady Elizabeth by the hand. He was considerably relieved when he saw Lady Elizabeth, because of her he was not afraid. "I do not at all mind waiting," he said. "How is Sir Harry?"

"Quite well."

"And yourself?"

"Pretty well, thank you."

"And Emily?"

Lady Elizabeth knew that in answering him she ought to call her own daughter Miss Hotspur, but she lacked the courage. "Emily is well too. Sir Harry has thought it best that I should come to you and explain that just at present he cannot ask you to Humblethwaite."

"I did not expect it."

"And he had rather not see you himself,—at least not here." Lady Elizabeth had not been instructed to propose a meeting. She had been told rather to avoid it if possible. But, like some other undiplomatic ambassadors, in her desire to be civil, she ran at once to the extremity of the permitted concessions. "If you have anything to say to Sir Harry—"

"I have, Lady Elizabeth; a great deal."

"And if you could write it—"

"I am so bad at writing."

"Then Sir Harry will go over and see you to-morrow at Penrith."

"That will be so very troublesome to him!"

"You need not regard that. At what hour shall he come?"

Cousin George was profuse in declaring that he would be at his cousin's disposal at any hour Sir Harry might select, from six in the morning throughout the day and night. But might he not say a word to Emily? At this proposition Lady Elizabeth shook her head vigorously. It was quite out of the question.

Circumstanced as they all were at present, Sir Harry would not
think of such a thing. And then it would do no good. Lady
Elizabeth did not believe that Emily herself would wish it. At
any rate there need be no further talk about it, as any such
interview was at present quite impossible. By all which
arguments and refusals, and the tone in which they were
pronounced, Cousin George was taught to perceive that, at any
rate in the mind of Lady Elizabeth, the process of parental
yielding had already commenced.

On all such occasions interviews are bad. The teller of
this story ventures to take the opportunity of recommending
parents in such cases always to refuse interviews, not only
between the young lady and the lover who is to be excluded, but
also between themselves and the lover. The vacillating tone,—
even when the resolve to suppress vacillation has been most
determined,—is perceived and understood, and at once utilized,
by the least argumentative of lovers, even by lovers who are
obtuse. The word "never" may be so pronounced as to make the
young lady's twenty thousand pounds full present value for ten
in the lover's pocket. There should be no arguments, no letters,
no interviews; and the young lady's love should be starved by
the absence of all other mention of the name, and by the
imperturbable good humour on all other matters of those with
whom she comes in contact in her own domestic circle. If it be
worth anything, it won't be starved; but if starving to death be
possible, that is the way to starve it. Lady Elizabeth was a bad
ambassador; and Cousin George, when he took his leave,
promising to be ready to meet Sir Harry at twelve on the
morrow, could almost comfort himself with a prospect of
success. He might be successful, if only he could stave off the
Walker and Bullbean portion of Mr. Hart's persecution! For he
understood that the success of his views at Humblethwaite must
postpone the payment by Sir Harry of those moneys for which
Mr. Hart and Captain Stubber were so unreasonably greedy. He
would have dared to defy the greed, but for the Walker and

Bullbean portion of the affair. Sir Harry already knew that he was in debt to these men; already knew with fair accuracy the amount of those debts. Hart and Stubber could not make him worse in Sir Harry's eyes than he was already, unless the Walker and Bullbean story should be told with the purpose of destroying him. How he did hate Walker and Bullbean and the memory of that evening;—and yet the money which now enabled him to drink champagne at the Penrith Crown was poor Mr. Walker's money! As he was driven back to Penrith he thought of all this, for some moments sadly, and at others almost with triumph. Might not a letter to Mr. Hart, with perhaps a word of truth in it, do some good? That evening, after his champagne, he wrote a letter:—

> DEAR MR. HART,—
>
> Things are going uncommon well here, only I hope you will do nothing to disturb just at present. It *must* come off, if a little time is given, and then *every shilling* will be paid. A few pounds more or less won't make any difference. Do arrange this, and you'll find I'll never forget how kind you have been. I've been at Humblethwaite to-day, and things are going quite smooth.
>
> Yours most sincerely,
>
> GEORGE HOTSPUR.
>
> Don't mention Walker's name, and everything shall be settled just as you shall fix.
>
> *The Crown, Penrith, Thursday.*

The moment the letter was written he rang the bell and gave it to the waiter. Such was the valour of drink operating on him now, as it had done when he wrote that other letter to Sir Harry! The drink made him brave to write, and to make attempts, and to dare consequences; but even whilst brave with drink, he knew that the morning's prudence would refuse its assent to such courage; and therefore, to save himself from the effects of the morning's cowardice, he put the letter at once out of his own power of control. After this fashion were arranged most of Cousin George's affairs. Before dinner on that day the evening of which he had passed with Mr. Walker, he had resolved that certain hints given to him by Mr. Bullbean should be of no avail to him;—not to that had he yet descended, nor would he so descend;—but with his brandy after dinner divine courage had come, and success had attended the brave. As soon as he was awake on that morning after writing to Mr. Hart, he rang his bell to inquire whether that letter which he had given to the waiter at twelve o'clock last night were still in the house. It was too late. The letter in which so imprudent a mention had been made of Mr. Walker's name was already in the post. "Never mind," said Cousin George to himself; "None but the brave deserve the fair." Then he turned round for another nap. It was not much past nine, and Sir Harry would not be there before twelve.

In the mean time there had been hope also and doubt also at Humblethwaite. Sir Harry was not surprised and hardly disappointed when he was told that he was to go to Penrith to see his cousin. The offer had been made by himself, and he was sure that he would not escape with less; and when Emily was told by her mother of the arrangement, she saw in it a way to the fulfilment of the prayer which she had made to her father. She would say nothing to him that evening, leaving to him the opportunity of speaking to her, should he choose to do so. But on the following morning she would repeat her prayer. On that evening not a word was said about George while Sir Harry and Lady Elizabeth were together with their daughter. Emily had made her plan, and she clung to it. Her father was very gentle with her, sitting close to her as she played some pieces of music to him in the evening, caressing her and looking lovingly into her eyes, as he bade God bless her when she left him for the night; but he had determined to say nothing to encourage her. He was still minded that there could be no such encouragement; but he doubted;—in his heart of hearts he doubted. He would still have bought off Cousin George by the sacrifice of half his property, and yet he doubted. After all, there would be some consolation in that binding together of the name and the property.

"What will you say to him?" Lady Elizabeth asked her husband that night.

"Tell him to go away."

"Nothing more than that?"

"What more is there to say? If he be willing to be bought, I will buy him. I will pay his debts and give him an income."

"You think, then, there can be no hope?"

"Hope!—for whom?"

"For Emily."

"I hope to preserve her—from a—scoundrel." And yet he had thought of the consolation!

Emily was very persistent in carrying out her plan. Prayers at Humblethwaite were always read with admirable punctuality at a quarter-past nine, so that breakfast might be commenced at half-past. Sir Harry every week-day was in his own room for three-quarters of an hour before prayers. All this was like clock-work at Humblethwaite. There would always be some man or men with Sir Harry during these three-quarters of an hour,—a tenant, a gamekeeper, a groom, a gardener, or a bailiff. But Emily calculated that if she made her appearance and held her ground, the tenant or the bailiff would give way, and that thus she would ensure a private interview with her father. Were she to wait till after breakfast, this would be difficult. A very few minutes after the half-hour she knocked at the door and was admitted. The village blacksmith was then suggesting a new smithy.

"Papa," said Emily, "if you would allow me half a minute—"

The village blacksmith and the bailiff, who was also present, withdrew, bowing to Emily, who gave to each of them a smile and a nod. They were her old familiar friends, and they looked kindly at her. She was to be their future lady; but was it not all important that their future lord should be a Hotspur?

Sir Harry had thought it not improbable that his daughter would come to him, but would have preferred to avoid the interview if possible. Here it was, however, and could not be avoided.

"Papa," she said, kissing him, "you are going to Penrith to-day."

"Yes, my dear."

"To see Cousin George?"

"Yes, Emily."

"Will you remember what we were saying the other day;—what I said?"

"I will endeavour to do my duty as best I may," said Sir Harry, after a pause.

"I am sure you will, Papa;—and so do I. I do endeavour to do my duty. Will you not try to help him?"

"Certainly, I will try to help him; for your sake rather than for his own. If I can help him with money, by paying his debts and giving him means to live, I will do so."

"Papa, that is not what I mean."

"What else can I do?"

"Save him from the evil of his ways."

"I will try. I would,—if I knew how,—even if only for the name's sake."

"For my sake also, Papa. Papa, let us do it together; you and I and Mamma. Let him come here."

"It is impossible."

"Let him come here," she said, as though disregarding his refusal. "You need not be afraid of me. I know how much there is to do that will be very hard in doing before any,—any other arrangement can be talked about."

"I am not afraid of you, my child."

"Let him come, then."

"No;—it would do no good. Do you think he would live here quietly?"

"Try him."

"What would people say?"

"Never mind what people would say: he is our cousin; he is your heir. He is the person whom I love best in all the world. Have you not a right to have him here if you wish it? I know what you are thinking of; but, Papa, there can never be anybody else;—never."

"Emily, you will kill me, I think."

"Dear Papa, let us see if we cannot try. And, oh, Papa, pray, pray let me see him." When she went away the bailiff and the blacksmith returned; but Sir Harry's power of resistance was gone, so that he succumbed to the new smithy without a word.

Chapter XX.

Cousin George's Success.

Thoughts crowded quick into the mind of Sir Harry Hotspur as he had himself driven over to Penrith. It was a dull, dreary day in November, and he took the close carriage. The distance was about ten miles, and he had therefore something above an hour for thinking. When men think much, they can rarely decide. The affairs as to which a man has once acknowledged to himself that he may be either wise or foolish, prudent or imprudent, are seldom matters on which he can by any amount of thought bring himself to a purpose which to his own eyes shall be clearly correct. When he can decide without thinking, then he can decide without a doubt, and with perfect satisfaction. But in this matter Sir Harry thought much. There had been various times at which he was quite sure that it was his duty to repudiate this cousin utterly. There had never been a time at which he had been willing to accept him. Nevertheless, at this moment, with all his struggles of thought he could not resolve. Was his higher duty due to his daughter, or to his family,—and through his family to his country, which, as he believed, owed its security and glory to the maintenance of its aristocracy? Would he be justified,—justified in any degree,—in subjecting his child to danger in the hope that his name and family pride might be maintained? Might he take his own desires in that direction as any make-weight towards a compliance with his girl's strong wishes, grounded as they were on quite other reasons? Mr. Boltby had been very eager in telling him that he ought to have nothing to say to this cousin, had loaded the cousin's name with every imaginable evil epithet; and of Mr. Boltby's truth and honesty there could be no doubt. But then Mr. Boltby had certainly exceeded his duty, and was of course disposed, by his professional view of the matter, to think any step the wisest which would tend to save the property from dangerous hands. Sir Harry felt that there were things to be saved of more value than the property;—the family, the title, perhaps that reprobate cousin himself; and then, above all, his child. He did believe that his child would not smile for him again, unless he would consent to make some effort in favour of her lover.

Doubtless the man was very bad. Sir Harry was sick at heart as he thought of the evil nature of the young man's vices. Of a man debauched in his life, extravagant with his money, even of a gambler, a drunkard, one fond of low men and of low women;—of one even such as this there might be hope, and the vicious man, if he will give up his vices, may still be loved and at last respected. But of a liar, a swindler, one mean as well as vicious, what hope could there be? It was essential to Sir Harry that the husband of his daughter should at any rate be a gentleman. The man's blood, indeed, was good; and blood will show at last, let the mud be ever so deep. So said Sir Harry to himself. And Emily would consent that the man should be tried by what severest fire might be kindled for the trying of him. If there were any gold there, it might be possible to send the dross adrift, and to get the gold without alloy. Could Lady Altringham have read Sir Harry's mind as his carriage was pulled up, just at twelve o'clock, at the door of the Penrith Crown, she would have been stronger than ever in her belief that young lovers, if they be firm, can always conquer opposing parents.

But alas, alas, there was no gold with this dross, and in that matter of blood, as to which Sir Harry's ideas were so strong, and indeed so noble, he entertained but a muddled theory. Noblesse oblige. High position will demand, and will often exact, high work. But that rule holds as good with a Buonaparte as with a Bourbon, with a Cromwell as with a Stewart; and succeeds as often and fails as often with the low born as with the high. And good blood too will have its effect,— physical for the most part,—and will produce bottom, lasting courage, that capacity of carrying on through the mud to which Sir Harry was wont to allude; but good blood will bring no man back to honesty. The two things together, no doubt, assist in producing the highest order of self-denying man.

When Sir Harry got out of his carriage, he had not yet made up his mind. The waiter had been told that he was expected, and showed him up at once into the large sitting-room looking out into the street, which Cousin George had bespoke for the occasion. He had had a smaller room himself, but had been smoking there, and at this moment in that room there was a decanter and a wine-glass on the chiffonier in one corner. He had heard the bustle of the arrival, and had at once gone into the saloon prepared for the reception of the great man. "I am so sorry to give you this trouble," said Cousin George, coming forward to greet his cousin. Sir Harry could not refuse his cousin's hand, though he would willingly have done so, had it been possible. "I should not mind the trouble," he said, "if it were of any use. I fear it can be of none."

"I hope you will not be prejudiced against me, Sir Harry."

"I trust that I am not prejudiced against any one. What is it that you wish me to do?"

"I want permission to go to Humblethwaite, as a suitor for your daughter's hand." So far Cousin George had prepared his speech beforehand.

"And what have you to recommend you to a father for such permission? Do you not know, sir, that when a gentleman proposes to a lady it is his duty to show that he is in a condition fit for the position which he seeks; that in character, in means, in rank, in conduct, he is at least her equal."

"As for our rank, Sir Harry, it is the same."

"And for your means? You know that my daughter is my heiress?"

"I do; but it is not that that has brought me to her. Of course, I have nothing. But then, you know, though she will inherit the estates, I must inherit—"

"If you please, sir, we will not go into all that again," said Sir Harry, interrupting him. "I explained to you before, sir, that I would have admitted your future rank as a counterpoise to her fortune, if I could have trusted your character. I cannot trust it. I do not know why you should thrust upon me the necessity of saying all this again. As I believe that you are in pecuniary distress, I made you an offer which I thought to be liberal."

"It was liberal, but it did not suit me to accept it." George had an inkling of what would pass within Sir Harry's bosom as to the acceptance or rejection of that offer. "I wrote to you, declining it, and as I have received no answer, I thought that I would just run down. What was I to do?"

"Do? How can I tell? Pay your debts. The money was offered you."

"I cannot give up my cousin. Has she been allowed to receive the letter which I left for her yesterday?"

Now Sir Harry had doubted much in his own mind as to the letter. During that morning's interview it had still been in his own possession. As he was preparing to leave the house he had made up his mind that she should have it; and Lady Elizabeth had been commissioned to give it her, not without instruction and explanation. Her father would not keep it from her, because he trusted her implicitly; but she was to understand that it could mean nothing to her, and that the letter must not of course be answered.

"It does not matter whether she did or did not," said Sir Harry. "I ask you again, whether you will accept the offer made you by Mr. Boltby, and give me your written promise not to renew this suit."

"I cannot do that, Sir Harry."

Sir Harry did not know how to proceed with the interview. As he had come there, some proposition must be made by himself. Had he intended to be altogether obstinate he should have remained at Humblethwaite, and kept his cousin altogether out of the house. And now his daughter's prayers were ringing in his ears: "Dear Papa, let us see if we cannot try." And then again that assurance which she had made him so solemnly: "Papa, there never can be anybody else!" If the black sheep could be washed white, the good of such washing would on every side be so great! He would have to blush,—let the washing be ever so perfect,—he must always blush in having such a son-in-law; but he had been forced to acknowledge to himself of late, that there was infinitely more of trouble and shame in this world than of joy or honour. Was it not in itself a disgrace that a Hotspur should do such things as this cousin had done; and a disgrace also that his daughter should have loved a man so unfit to be her lover? And then from day to day, and from hour to hour, he remembered that these ills were added to the death of that son, who, had he lived, would have been such a glory to him. More of trouble and disgrace! Was it not all trouble and disgrace? He would have wished that the day might come for him to go away and leave it all, were it not that for one placed as he was placed his own life would not see the end of these troubles. He must endeavour to provide that everything should not go to utter ruin as soon as he should have taken his departure.

He walked about the room, again trying to think. Or, perhaps, all thinking was over with him now, and he was resolving in his own mind how best he might begin to yield. He must obey his daughter. He could not break the heart of the only child that was left to him. He had no delight in the world other than what came to him reflected back from her. He felt now as though he was simply a steward endeavouring on her behalf to manage things to the best advantage; but still only a steward, and as such only a servant who could not at last decide on the mode of management to be adopted. He could endeavour to persuade, but she must decide. Now his daughter had decided, and he must begin this task, so utterly distasteful to him, of endeavouring to wash the blackamoor white.

"What are you willing to do?" he asked.

"How to do, Sir Harry?"

"You have led a bad life."

"I suppose I have, Sir Harry."

"How will you show yourself willing to reform it?"

"Only pay my debts and set me up with ready money, and I'll go along as slick as grease!" Thus would Cousin George have answered the question had he spoken his mind freely. But he knew that he might not be so explicit. He must promise much; but, of course, in making his promise he must arrange about his debts. "I'll do almost anything you like. Only try me. Of course it would be so much easier if those debts were paid off. I'll give up races altogether, if you mean that, Sir Harry. Indeed, I'm ready to give up anything."

"Will you give up London?"

"London!" In simple truth, George did not quite understand the proposition.

"Yes; will you leave London? Will you go and live at Scarrowby, and learn to look after the farm and the place?"

George's face fell,—his face being less used to lying than his tongue; but his tongue lied at once: "Oh yes, certainly, if you wish it. I should rather like a life of that sort. For how long would it be?"

"For two years," said Sir Harry, grimly.

Cousin George, in truth, did not understand. He thought that he was to take his bride with him when he went to Scarrowby. "Perhaps Emily would not like it," he said.

"It is what she desires. You do not suppose that she knows so little of your past life as to be willing to trust herself into your hands at once. She is attached to you."

"And so am I to her; on my honour I am. I'm sure you don't doubt that."

Sir Harry doubted every word that fell from his cousin's mouth, but still he persevered. He could perceive though he could not analyse, and there was hardly a tone which poor Cousin George used which did not discourage the Baronet. Still he persevered. He must persevere now, even if it were only to prove to Emily how much of basest clay and how little of gold there was in this image.

"She is attached to you," he continued, "and you bear our name, and will be the head of our family. If you will submit yourself to a reformed life, and will prove that you are fit for her, it may be possible that after years she should be your wife."

"After years, Sir Harry?"

"Yes, sir,—after years. Do you suppose that the happiness of such an one as she can be trusted to such keeping as yours without a trial of you? You will find that she has no such hope herself."

"Oh, of course; what she likes—"

"I will pay your debts; on condition that Mr. Boltby is satisfied that he has the entire list of them."

George, as he heard this, at once determined that he must persuade Mr. Hart to include Mr. Walker's little account in that due to himself. It was only a matter of a few hundreds, and might surely be arranged when so much real money would be passing from hand to hand.

"I will pay everything; you shall then go down to Scarrowby, and the house shall be prepared for you."

It wasn't supposed, George thought, that he was absolutely to live in solitary confinement at Scarrowby. He might have a friend or two, and then the station was very near.

"You are fond of shooting, and you will have plenty of it there. We will get you made a magistrate for the county, and there is much to do in looking after the property." Sir Harry became almost good-humoured in his tone as he described the kind of life which he intended that the blackamoor should live. "We will come to you for a month each year, and then you can come to us for a while."

"When shall it begin?" asked Cousin George, as soon as the Baronet paused. This was a question difficult to be answered. In fact, the arrangement must be commenced at once. Sir Harry knew very well that, having so far yielded, he must take his cousin back with him to Humblethwaite. He must keep his cousin now in his possession till all those debts should be paid, and till the house at Scarrowby should be prepared; and he must trust to his daughter's prudence and high sense of right not to treat her lover with too tender an acknowledgment of her love till he should have been made to pass through the fire of reform.

"You had better get ready and come back to Humblethwaite with me now," said Sir Harry.

Within five minutes after that there was bustling about the passages and hall of the Crown Hotel. Everybody in the house, from the august landlord down to the humble stableboy, knew that there had been a reconciliation between Sir Harry and his cousin, and that the cousin was to be made welcome to all the good the gods could give. While Cousin George was packing his things, Sir Harry called for the bill and paid it,—without looking at it, because he would not examine how the blackamoor had lived while he was still a blackamoor.

"I wonder whether he observed the brandy," thought Cousin George to himself.

Chapter XXI.

Emily Hotspur's Sermon.

The greater portion of the journey back to Humblethwaite was passed in silence. Sir Harry had undertaken an experiment in which he had no faith himself, and was sad at heart. Cousin George was cowed, half afraid, and yet half triumphant. Could it be possible that he should "pull through" after all? Some things had gone so well with him. His lady friends had been so true to him! Lady Altringham, and then Mrs. Morton,—how good they had been! Dear Lucy! He would never forget her. And Emily was such a brick! He was going to see his Emily, and that would be "so jolly." Nevertheless, he did acknowledge to himself that an Emily prepared to assist her father in sending her lover through the fire of reform, would not be altogether "so jolly" as the Emily who had leaned against him on the bridge at Airey Force, while his arm had been tightly clasped round her waist. He was alive to the fact that romance must give place to business.

When they had entered the park-gates, Sir Harry spoke. "You must understand, George"—he had not called him George before since the engagement had been made known to him— "that you cannot yet be admitted here as my daughter's accepted suitor, as might have been the case had your past life been different."

"I see all that," said Cousin George.

"It is right that I should tell you so; but I trust implicitly to Emily's high sense of duty and propriety. And now that you are here, George, I trust that it may be for your advantage and for ours."

Then he pressed his cousin's hand, if not with affection, at least with sincerity.

"I'm sure it is to be all right now," said George, calculating whether he would be able to escape to London for a few days, so that he might be able to arrange that little matter with Mr. Hart. They couldn't suppose that he would be able to leave London for two years without a day's notice!

Sir Harry got out of the carriage at the front door, and desired Cousin George to follow him into the house. He turned at once into the small room where George had drunk the sherry, and desired that Lady Elizabeth might be sent to him.

"My dear," said he, "I have brought George back with me. We will do the best that we can. Mrs. Quick will have a room for him. You had better tell Emily, and let her come to me for a moment before she sees her cousin." This was all said in George's hearing. And then Sir Harry went, leaving his cousin in the hands of Lady Elizabeth.

"I am glad to see you back again, George," she said, with a melancholy voice.

Cousin George smiled, and said, that "it would be all right."

"I am sure I hope so, for my girl's sake. But there must be a great change, George."

"No end of a change," said Cousin George, who was not in the least afraid of Lady Elizabeth.

Many things of moment had to be done in the house that day before dinner. In the first place there was a long interview between the father and daughter. For a few minutes, perhaps, he was really happy when she was kneeling with her arms upon his knees, thanking him for what he had done, while tears of joy were streaming down her cheeks. He would not bring himself to say a word of caution to her. Would it not be to paint the snow white to caution her as to her conduct?

"I have done as you bade me in everything," he said. "I have proposed to him that he should go to Scarrowby. It may be that it will be your home for a while, dear."

She thanked him and kissed him again and again. She would be so good. She would do all she could to deserve his kindness. And as for George,—"Pray, Papa, don't think that I suppose that it can be all done quite at once." Nevertheless it was in that direction that her thoughts erred. It did seem to her that the hard part of the work was already done, and that now the pleasant paths of virtue were to be trod with happy and persistent feet.

"You had better see him in your mother's presence, dearest, before dinner; and then the awkwardness will be less afterwards."

She kissed him again, and ran from his room up to her mother's apartment, taking some back stairs well known to herself, lest she should by chance meet her lover after some undue and unprepared fashion. And there she could sit down and think of it all! She would be very discreet. He should be made to understand at once that the purgation must be thorough, the reform complete. She would acknowledge her love to him,—her great and abiding love; but of lover's tenderness there could be but little,—almost none,—till the fire had done its work, and the gold should have been separated from the dross. She had had her way so far, and they should find that she had deserved it.

Before dinner Sir Harry wrote a letter to his lawyer. The mail-cart passed through the village on its way to Penrith late in the evening, and there was time for him to save the post. He thought it incumbent on him to let Mr. Boltby know that he had changed his mind; and, though the writing of the letter was not

an agreeable task, he did it at once. He said nothing to Mr.
Boltby directly about his daughter, but he made it known to that
gentleman that Cousin George was at present a guest at
Humblethwaite, and that he intended to pay all the debts without
entering into any other specific engagements. Would Mr. Boltby
have the goodness to make out a schedule of the debts? Captain
Hotspur should be instructed to give Mr. Boltby at once all the
necessary information by letter. Then Sir Harry went on to say
that perhaps the opinions formed in reference to Captain Hotspur
had been too severe. He was ashamed of himself as he wrote
these words, but still they were written. If the blackamoor was to
be washed white, the washing must be carried out at all times, at
all seasons, and in every possible manner, till the world should
begin to see that the blackness was going out of the skin.

Cousin George was summoned to meet the girl who
loved him in her mother's morning-room, before they dressed
for dinner. He did not know at all in what way to conduct
himself. He had not given a moment's thought to it till the
difficulty flashed upon him as she entered the apartment. But she
had considered it all. She came up to him quickly, and gave him
her lips to kiss, standing there in her mother's presence.

"George," she said, "dear George! I am so glad that you
are here."

It was the first; and it should be the last,—till the fire had
done its work; till the fire should at least have done so much of
its work as to make the remainder easy and fairly sure. He had
little to say for himself, but muttered something about his being
the happiest fellow in the world. It was a position in which a
man could hardly behave well, and neither the mother nor the
daughter expected much from him. A man cannot bear himself
gracefully under the weight of a pardon as a woman may do. A
man chooses generally that it shall be assumed by those with
whom he is closely connected that he has done and is doing no
wrong; and, when wronged, he professes to forgive and to forget
in silence. To a woman the act of forgiveness, either accepted or

bestowed, is itself a pleasure. A few words were then spoken, mostly by Lady Elizabeth, and the three separated to prepare for dinner.

The next day passed over them at Humblethwaite Hall very quietly, but with some mild satisfaction. Sir Harry told his cousin of the letter to his lawyer, and desired George to make out and send by that day's post such a schedule as might be possible on the spur of the moment.

"Hadn't I better run up and see Mr. Boltby?" said Cousin George.

But to this Sir Harry was opposed. Let any calls for money reach them there. Whatever the calls might be, he at any rate could pay them. Cousin George repeated his suggestion; but acquiesced when Sir Harry frowned and showed his displeasure. He did make out a schedule, and did write a letter to Mr. Boltby.

"I think my debt to Mr. Hart was put down as £3,250," he wrote, "but I believe I should have added another £350 for a transaction as to which I fancy he does not hold my note of hand. But the money is due."

He was fool enough to think that Mr. Walker's claim might be liquidated after this fashion. In the afternoon they rode together,—the father, the daughter, and the blackamoor, and much was told to Cousin George as to the nature of the property. The names of the tenants were mentioned, and the boundaries of the farms were pointed out to him. He was thinking all the time whether Mr. Hart would spare him.

But Emily Hotspur, though she had been thus reticent and quiet in her joy, though she was resolved to be discreet, and knew that there were circumstances in her engagement which would for a while deter her from being with her accepted lover as other girls are with theirs, did not mean to estrange herself from her cousin George. If she were to do so, how was she to assist, and take, as she hoped to do, the first part in that task of refining the gold on which they were all now intent? She was to correspond with him when he was at Scarrowby. Such was her present programme, and Sir Harry had made no objection when she declared her purpose. Of course they must understand each other, and have communion together. On the third day, therefore, it was arranged they two should walk, without other company, about the place. She must show him her own gardens, which were at some distance from the house. If the truth be told, it must be owned that George somewhat dreaded the afternoon's amusement; but had she demanded of him to sit down to listen to her while she read to him a sermon, he would not have refused.

To be didactic and at the same time demonstrative of affection is difficult, even with mothers towards their children, though with them the assumption of authority creates no sense of injury. Emily specially desired to point out to the erring one the paths of virtue, and yet to do so without being oppressive.

"It is so nice to have you here, George," she said.

"Yes, indeed; isn't it?" He was walking beside her, and as yet they were within view of the house.

"Papa has been so good; isn't he good?"

"Indeed he is. The best man I know out," said George, thinking that his gratitude would have been stronger had the Baronet given him the money and allowed him to go up to London to settle his own debts.

"And Mamma has been so kind! Mamma is very fond of you. I am sure she would do anything for you."

"And you?" said George, looking into her face.

"I!—As for me, George, it is a matter of course now. You do not want to be told again what is and ever must be my first interest in the world."

"I do not care how often you tell me."

"But you know it; don't you?"

"I know what you said at the waterfall, Emily."

"What I said then I said for always. You may be sure of that. I told Mamma so, and Papa. If they had not wanted me to love you, they should not have asked you to come here. I do love you, and I hope that some day I may be your wife."

She was not leaning on his arm, but as she spoke she stopped, and looked steadfastly into his face. He put out his hand as though to take hers; but she shook her head, refusing it. "No, George; come on. I want to talk to you a great deal. I want to say ever so much,—now, to-day. I hope that some day I may be your wife. If I am not, I shall never be any man's wife."

"What does some day mean, Emily?"

"Ever so long;—years, perhaps."

"But why? A fellow has to be consulted, you know, as well as yourself. What is the use of waiting? I know Sir Harry thinks I have been very fond of pleasure. How can I better show him how willing I am to give it up than by marrying and settling down at once? I don't see what's to be got by waiting?"

Of course she must tell him the truth. She had no idea of keeping back the truth. She loved him with all her heart, and was resolved to marry him; but the dross must first be purged from the gold. "Of course you know, George, that Papa has made objections."

"I know he did, but that is over now. I am to go and live at Scarrowby at once, and have the shooting. He can't want me to remain there all by myself."

"But he does; and so do I."

"Why?"

In order that he might be made clean by the fire of solitude and the hammer of hard work. She could not quite say this to him. "You know, George, your life has been one of pleasure."

"I was in the army,—for some years."

"But you left it, and you took to going to races, and they say that you gambled and are in debt, and you have been reckless. Is not that true, George?"

"It is true."

"And should you wonder that Papa should be afraid to trust his only child and all his property to one who,—who knows that he has been reckless? But if you can show, for a year or two, that you can give up all that—"

"Wouldn't it be all given up if we were married?"

"Indeed, I hope so. I should break my heart otherwise. But can you wonder that Papa should wish for some delay and some proof?"

"Two years!"

"Is that much? If I find you doing what he wishes, these two years will be so happy to me! We shall come and see you, and you will come here. I have never liked Scarrowby, because it is not pretty, as this place is; but, oh, how I shall like to go there now! And when you are here, Papa will get to be so fond of you. You will be like a real son to him. Only you must be steady."

"Steady! by Jove, yes. A fellow will have to be steady at Scarrowby." The perfume of the cleanliness of the life proposed to him was not sweet to his nostrils.

She did not like this, but she knew that she could not have everything at once. "You must know," she said, "that there is a bargain between me and Papa. I told him that I should tell you everything."

"Yes; I ought to be told everything."

"It is he that shall fix the day. He is to do so much, that he has a right to that. I shall never press him, and you must not."

"Oh, but I shall."

"It will be of no use; and, George, I won't let you. I shall scold you if you do. When he thinks that you have learned how to manage the property, and that your mind is set upon that kind of work, and that there are no more races,—mind, and no betting, then,—then he will consent. And I will tell you something more if you would like to hear it."

"Something pleasant, is it?"

"When he does, and tells me that he is not afraid to give me to you, I shall be the happiest girl in all England. Is that pleasant?—No, George, no; I will not have it."

"Not give me one kiss?"

"I gave you one when you came, to show you that in truth I loved you. I will give you another when Papa says that everything is right."

"Not till then?"

"No, George, not till then. But I shall love you just the same. I cannot love you better than I do."

He had nothing for it but to submit, and was obliged to be content during the remainder of their long walk with talking of his future life at Scarrowby. It was clearly her idea that he should be head-farmer, head-steward, head-accountant, and general workman for the whole place. When he talked about the game, she brought him back to the plough;—so at least he declared to himself. And he could elicit no sympathy from her when he reminded her that the nearest meet of hounds was twenty miles and more from Scarrowby. "You can think of other things for a while," she said. He was obliged to say that he would, but it did seem to him that Scarrowby was a sort of penal servitude to which he was about to be sent with his own concurrence. The scent of the cleanliness was odious to him.

"I don't know what I shall do there of an evening," he said.

"Read," she answered; "there are lots of books, and you can always have the magazines. I will send them to you." It was a very dreary prospect of life for him, but he could not tell her that it would be absolutely unendurable.

When their walk was over,—a walk which she never could forget, however long might be her life, so earnest had been her purpose,—he was left alone, and took another stroll by himself. How would it suit him? Was it possible? Could the event "come off"? Might it not have been better for him had he allowed his other loving friend to prepare for him the letter to the Baronet, in which Sir Harry's munificent offer would have been accepted? Let us do him the justice to remember that he was quite incapable of understanding the misery, the utter ruin which that letter would have entailed upon her who loved him so well. He knew nothing of such sufferings as would have been hers—as must be hers, for had she not already fallen haplessly into the pit when she had once allowed herself to fix her heart upon a thing so base as this? It might have been better, he thought, if that letter had been written. A dim dull idea came upon him that he was not fit to be this girl's husband. He could not find his joys where she would find hers. No doubt it would be a grand thing to own Humblethwaite and Scarrowby at some future time; but Sir Harry might live for these twenty years, and while Sir Harry lived he must be a slave. And then he thought that upon the whole he liked Lucy Morton better than Emily Hotspur. He could say what he chose to Lucy, and smoke in her presence, own that he was fond of drink, and obtain some sympathy for his "book" on the Derby. He began to feel already that he did not like sermons from the girl of his heart.

But he had chosen this side now, and he must go on with the game. It seemed certain to him that his debts would at any rate be paid. He was not at all certain how matters might go in reference to Mr. Walker, but if matters came to the worst the Baronet would probably be willing to buy him off again with the promised income. Nevertheless, he was not comfortable, and certainly did not shine at Sir Harry's table. "Why she has loved him, what she has seen in him, I cannot tell," said Sir Harry to his wife that night.

We must presume Sir Harry did not know how it is that the birds pair.

Chapter XXII.

George Hotspur Yields.

On the morning of Cousin George's fourth day at Humblethwaite, there came a letter for Sir Harry. The post reached the Hall about an hour before the time at which the family met for prayers, and the letters were taken into Sir Harry's room. The special letter of which mention is here made shall be given to the reader entire:—

—, *Lincoln's Inn Fields, 24th Nov. 186—.*

My Dear Sir Harry Hotspur,—

I have received your letter in reference to Captain Hotspur's debts, and have also received a letter from him, and a list of what he says he owes. Of course there can be no difficulty in paying all debts which he acknowledges, if you think proper to do so. As far as I am able to judge at present, the amount would be between twenty-five and thirty thousand pounds. I should say nearer the former than the latter sum, did I not know that the amount in such matters always goes on increasing. You must also understand that I cannot guarantee the correctness of this statement.

But I feel myself bound in my duty to go further than this, even though it may be at the risk of your displeasure. I presume from what you tell me that you are

contemplating a marriage between George Hotspur and
your daughter; and I now repeat to you, in the most solemn
words that I can use, my assurance that the marriage is one
which you should not countenance. Captain Hotspur is not
fit to marry your daughter.

When Sir Harry had read so far he had become very angry, but
his anger was now directed against his lawyer. Had he not told
Mr. Boltby that he had changed his mind; and what business had
the lawyer to interfere with him further? But he read the letter on
to its bitter end:—

Since you were in London the following facts have become
known to me. On the second of last month Mr. George
Hotspur met two men, named Walker and Bullbean, in the
lodgings of the former, at about nine in the evening, and
remained there during the greater part of the night, playing
cards. Bullbean is a man well known to the police as a card-
sharper. He once moved in the world as a gentleman. His
trade is now to tout and find prey for gamblers. Walker is a
young man in a low rank of life, who had some money.
George Hotspur on that night won between three and four
hundred pounds of Walker's money; and Bullbean, over
and above this, got for himself some considerable amount
of plunder. Walker is now prepared, and very urgent, to
bring the circumstances of this case before a magistrate,
having found out, or been informed, that some practice of
cheating was used against him; and Bullbean is ready to
give evidence as to George Hotspur's foul play. They have
hitherto been restrained by Hart, the Jew whom you met.
Hart fears that were the whole thing made public, his bills
would not be taken up by you.

I think that I know all this to be true. If you
conceive that I am acting in a manner inimical to your
family, you had better come up to London and put yourself
into the hands of some other lawyer. If you can still trust
me, I will do the best I can for you. I should recommend
you to bring Captain Hotspur with you,—if he will come.

I grieve to write as I have done, but it seems to me
that no sacrifice is too great to make with the object of
averting the fate to which, as I fear, Miss Hotspur is
bringing herself.

—My dear Sir Harry Hotspur,

I am, very faithfully yours,

JOHN BOLTBY.

It was a terrible letter! Gradually, as he read it and re-read it, there came upon Sir Harry the feeling that he might owe, that he did owe, that he certainly would owe to Mr. Boltby a very heavy debt of gratitude. Gradually the thin glazing of hope with which he had managed to daub over and partly to hide his own settled convictions as to his cousin's character fell away, and he saw the man as he had seen him during his interview with Captain Stubber and Mr. Hart. It must be so. Let the consequences be what they might, his daughter must be told. Were she to be killed by the telling, it would be better than that she should be handed over to such a man as this. The misfortune which had come upon them might be the death of him and of her;—but better that than the other. He sat in his chair till the gong sounded through the house for prayers; then he rang his bell and sent in word to Lady Elizabeth that she should read them in his absence. When they were over, word was brought that he would breakfast alone, in his own room. On receiving that message, both his wife and daughter went to him; but as yet he could tell them nothing. Tidings had come which would make it necessary that he should go at once to London. As soon as breakfast should be over he would see George Hotspur. They both knew from the tone in which the name was pronounced that the "tidings" were of their nature bad, and that they had reference to the sins of their guest.

"You had better read that letter," he said as soon as George was in the room. As he spoke his face was towards the fire, and in that position he remained. The letter had been in his hand, and he only half turned round to give it. George read the letter slowly, and when he had got through it, only half understanding the words, but still knowing well the charge which it contained, stood silent, utterly conquered. "I suppose it is true?" said Sir Harry, in a low voice, facing his enemy.

"I did win some money," said Cousin George.

"And you cheated?"

"Oh dear no;—nothing of the sort."

But his confession was written in his face, and was heard in his voice, and peeped out through every motion of his limbs. He was a cur, and denied the accusation in a currish manner, hardly intended to create belief.

"He must be paid back his money," said Sir Harry.

"I had promised that," said Cousin George.

"Has it been your practice, sir, when gambling, to pay back money that you have won? You are a scoundrel,—a heartless scoundrel,—to try and make your way into my house when I had made such liberal offers to buy your absence." To this Cousin George made no sort of answer. The game was up. And had he not already told himself that it was a game that he should never have attempted to play? "We will leave this house if you please, both of us, at eleven. We will go to town together. The carriage will be ready at eleven. You had better see to the packing of your things, with the servant."

"Shall I not say a word of adieu to Lady Elizabeth?"

"No, sir! You shall never speak to a female in my house again."

The two were driven over to Penrith together, and went up to London in the same carriage, Sir Harry paying for all expenses without a word. Sir Harry before he left his house saw his wife for a moment, but he did not see his daughter. "Tell her," said he, "that it must be,—must be all over." The decision was told to Emily, but she simply refused to accept it. "It shall not be so," said she, flashing out. Lady Elizabeth endeavoured to show her that her father had done all he could to further her views—had been ready to sacrifice to her all his own wishes and convictions.

"Why is he so changed? He has heard of some new debt. Of course there are debts. We did not suppose that it could be done all at once, and so easily." She refused to be comforted, and refused to believe. She sat alone weeping in her own room, and swore, when her mother came to her, that no consideration, no tidings as to George's past misconduct, should induce her to break her faith to the man to whom her word had been given;— "my word, and Papa's, and yours," said Emily, pleading her cause with majesty through her tears.

On the day but one following there came a letter from Sir Harry to Lady Elizabeth, very short, but telling her the whole truth. "He has cheated like a common low swindler as he is, with studied tricks at cards, robbing a poor man, altogether beneath him in station, of hundreds of pounds. There is no doubt about it. It is uncertain even yet whether he will not be tried before a jury. He hardly even denies it. A creature viler, more cowardly, worse, the mind of man cannot conceive. My broken-hearted, dearest, best darling must be told all this. Tell her that I know what she will suffer. Tell her that I shall be as crushed by it as she. But anything is better than degradation such as this. Tell her specially that I have not decided without absolute knowledge." Emily was told. The letter was read to her and by her till she knew it almost by heart. There came upon her a wan look of abject agony, that seemed to rob her at once of her youth and beauty; but even now she would not yield. She did not longer affect to disbelieve the tidings, but said that no man, let him do what he might, could be too far gone for repentance and forgiveness. She would wait. She had talked of waiting two years. She would be content to wait ten. What though he had cheated at cards! Had she not once told her mother that should it turn out that he had been a murderer, then she would become a murderer's wife? She did not know that cheating at cards was worse than betting at horse-races. It was all bad,—very bad. It was the kind of life into which men were led by the fault of those who should have taught them better. No; she would not marry him without her father's leave: but she would never own that her engagement was broken, let them affix what most opprobrious name to him they might choose. To her card-sharpers seemed to be no worse than gamblers. She was quite sure that Christ had come to save men who cheat at cards as well as others.

As Sir Harry and his cousin entered the London station late at night,—it was past midnight,—Sir Harry bade his companion meet him the next morning at Mr. Boltby's chambers at eleven. Cousin George had had ample time for meditation, and had considered that it might be best for him to "cut up a little rough."

"Mr. Boltby is my enemy," he said, "and I don't know what I am to get by going there."

"If you don't, sir, I'll not pay one shilling for you."

"I have your promise, Sir Harry."

"If you are not there at the time I fix, I will pay nothing, and the name may go to the dogs."

Then they both went to the station hotel,—not together, but the younger following the elder's feet,—and slept for the last time in their lives under one roof.

Cousin George did not show himself at Mr. Boltby's, being still in his bed at the station hotel at the time named; but at three o'clock he was with Mrs. Morton.

For the present we will go back to Sir Harry. He was at the lawyer's chambers at the time named, and Mr. Boltby smiled when told of the summons which had been given to Cousin George. By this time Sir Harry had acknowledged his gratitude to Mr. Boltby over and over again, and Mr. Boltby perhaps, having no daughter, thought that the evil had been cured. He was almost inclined to be jocular, and did laugh at Sir Harry in a mild way when told of the threat.

"We must pay his debts, Sir Harry, I think."

"I don't see it at all. I would rather face everything. And I told him that I would pay nothing."

"Ah, but you had told him that you would. And then those cormorants have been told so also. We had better build a bridge of gold for a falling enemy. Stick to your former proposition, without any reference to a legacy, and make him write the letter. My clerk shall find him to-morrow."

Sir Harry at last gave way; the lucky Walker received back his full money, Bullbean's wages of iniquity and all; and Sir Harry returned to Humblethwaite.

Cousin George was sitting in Mrs. Morton's room with a very bad headache five days after his arrival in London, and she was reading over a manuscript which she had just written. "That will do, I think," she said.

"Just the thing," said he, without raising his head.

"Will you copy it now, George?"

"Not just now, I am so seedy. I'll take it and do it at the club."

"No; I will not have that. The draft would certainly be left out on the club table; and you would go to billiards, and the letter never would be written."

"I'll come back and do it after dinner."

"I shall be at the theatre then, and I won't have you here in my absence. Rouse yourself and do it now. Don't be such a poor thing."

"That's all very well, Lucy; but if you had a sick headache, you wouldn't like to have to write a d———d letter like that."

Then she rose up to scold him, being determined that the letter should be written then and there. "Why, what a coward you are; what a feckless, useless creature! Do you think that I have never to go for hours on the stage, with the gas in a blaze around me, and my head ready to split? And what is this? A paper to write that will take you ten minutes. The truth is, you don't like to give up the girl!" Could she believe it of him after knowing him so well; could she think that there was so much of good in him?

"You say that to annoy me. You know that I never cared for her."

"You would marry her now if they would let you."

"No, by George. I've had enough of that. You're wide awake enough to understand, Lucy, that a fellow situated as I am, over head and ears in debt, and heir to an old title, should struggle to keep the things together. Families and names don't matter much, I suppose; but, after all, one does care for them. But I've had enough of that. As for Cousin Emily, you know, Lucy, I never loved any woman but you in my life."

He was a brute, unredeemed by any one manly gift; idle, self-indulgent, false, and without a principle. She was a woman greatly gifted, with many virtues, capable of self-sacrifice, industrious, affectionate, and loving truth if not always true herself. And yet such a word as that from this brute sufficed to please her for the moment. She got up and kissed his forehead and dropped for him some strong spirit in a glass, which she mixed with water, and cooled his brow with eau-de-cologne. "Try to write it, dearest. It should be written at once if it is to be written." Then he turned himself wearily to her writing-desk, and copied the words which she had prepared for him.

The letter was addressed to Mr. Boltby, and purported to be a renunciation of all claim to Miss Hotspur's hand, on the understanding that his debts were paid for him to the extent of £25,000, and that an allowance were made to him of £500 a year, settled on him as an annuity for life, as long as he should live out of England. Mr. Boltby had given him to understand that this clause would not be exacted, unless circumstances should arise which should make Sir Harry think it imperative upon him to demand its execution. The discretion must be left absolute with Sir Harry; but, as Mr. Boltby said, Captain Hotspur could trust Sir Harry's word and his honour.

"If I'm to be made to go abroad, what the devil are you to do?" he had said to Mrs. Morton.

"There need be no circumstances," said Mrs. Morton, "to make it necessary."

Of course Captain Hotspur accepted the terms on her advice. He had obeyed Lady Altringham, and had tried to obey Emily, and would now obey Mrs. Morton, because Mrs. Morton was the nearest to him.

The letter which he copied was a well-written letter, put together with much taste, so that the ignoble compact to which it gave assent should seem to be as little ignoble as might be possible. "I entered into the arrangement," the letter said in its last paragraph, "because I thought it right to endeavour to keep the property and the title together; but I am aware now that my position in regard to my debts was of a nature that should have deterred me from the attempt. As I have failed, I sincerely hope that my cousin may be made happy by some such splendid alliance as she is fully entitled to expect." He did not understand all that the words conveyed; but yet he questioned them. He did not perceive that they were intended to imply that the writer had never for a moment loved the girl whom he had proposed to marry. Nevertheless they did convey to him dimly some idea that they might give,—not pain, for as to that he would have been indifferent,—but offence. "Will there be any good in all that?" he asked.

"Certainly," said she. "You don't mean to whine and talk of your broken heart."

"Oh dear, no; nothing of that sort."

"This is the manly way to put it, regarding the matter simply as an affair of business."

"I believe it is," said he; and then, having picked himself up somewhat by the aid of a glass of sherry, he continued to copy the letter, and to direct it.

"I will keep the rough draft," said Mrs. Morton.

"And I must go now, I suppose," he said.

"You can stay here and see me eat my dinner if you like. I shall not ask you to share it, because it consists of two small mutton chops, and one wouldn't keep me up through Lady Teazle."

"I've a good mind to come and see you," said he.

"Then you'd better go and eat your own dinner at once."

"I don't care about my dinner. I should have a bit of supper afterwards."

Then she preached to him a sermon; not quite such a one as Emily Hotspur had preached, but much more practical, and with less reticence. If he went on living as he was living now, he would "come to grief." He was drinking every day, and would some day find that he could not do so with impunity. Did he know what delirium tremens was? Did he want to go to the devil altogether? Had he any hope as to his future life?

"Yes," said he, "I hope to make you my wife." She tossed her head, and told him that with all the will in the world to sacrifice herself, such sacrifice could do him no good if he persisted in making himself a drunkard. "But I have been so tried these last two months. If you only knew what Mr. Boltby and Captain Stubber and Sir Harry and Mr. Hart were altogether. Oh, my G——!" But he did not say a word about Messrs. Walker and Bullbean. The poor woman who was helping him knew nothing of Walker and Bullbean. Let us hope that she may remain in that ignorance.

Cousin George, before he left her, swore that he would amend his mode of life, but he did not go to see Lady Teazle that night. There were plenty of men now back in town ready to play pool at the club.

Chapter XXIII.

"I Shall Never Be Married."

Sir Harry Hotspur returned to Humblethwaite before Cousin George's letter was written, though when he did return all the terms had been arranged, and a portion of the money paid. Perhaps it would have been better that he should have waited and taken the letter with him in his pocket; but in truth he was so wretched that he could not wait. The thing was fixed and done, and he could but hurry home to hide his face among his own people. He felt that the glory of his house was gone from him. He would sit by the hour together thinking of the boy who had died. He had almost, on occasions, allowed himself to forget his boy, while hoping that his name and wide domains might be kept together by the girl that was left to him. He was beginning to understand now that she was already but little better than a wreck. Indeed, was not everything shipwreck around him? Was he not going to pieces on the rocks? Did not the lesson of every hour seem to tell him that, throughout his long life, he had thought too much of his house and his name?

It would have been better that he should have waited till the letter was in his pocket before he returned home, because, when he reached Humblethwaite, the last argument was wanting to him to prove to Emily that her hope was vain. Even after his arrival, when the full story was told to her, she held out in her resolve. She accepted the truth of that scene at Walker's rooms. She acknowledged that her lover had cheated the wretched man at cards. After that all other iniquities were of course as nothing. There was a completeness in that of which she did not fail to accept, and to use the benefit. When she had once taken it as true that her lover had robbed his inferior by foul play at cards, there could be no good in alluding to this or that lie, in counting up this or that disreputable debt, in alluding to habits of brandy-drinking, or even in soiling her pure mind with any word as to Mrs. Morton. It was granted that he was as vile as sin could make him. Had not her Saviour come exactly for such as this one, because of His great love for those who were vile; and should not her human love for one enable her to do that which His great heavenly love did always for all men? Every reader will know how easily answerable was the argument. Most readers will also know how hard it is to win by attacking the reason when the heart is the fortress that is in question. She had accepted his guilt, and why tell her of it any further? Did she not pine over his guilt, and weep for it day and night, and pray that he might yet be made white as snow? But guilty as he was, a poor piece of broken vilest clay, without the properties even which are useful to the potter, he was as dear to her as when she had leaned against him believing him to be a pillar of gold set about with onyx stones, jaspers, and rubies. There was but one sin on his part which could divide them. If, indeed, he should cease to love her, then there would be an end to it! It would have been better that Sir Harry should have remained in London till he could have returned with George's autograph letter in his pocket.

"You must have the letter in his own handwriting," Mr. Boltby had said, cunningly, "only you must return it to me."

Sir Harry had understood, and had promised, that the letter should be returned when it had been used for the cruel purpose for which it was to be sent to Humblethwaite. For all Sir Harry's own purposes Mr. Boltby's statements would have quite sufficed.

She was told that her lover would renounce her, but she would not believe what she was told. Of course he would accept the payment of his debts. Of course he would take an income when offered to him. What else was he to do? How was he to live decently without an income? All these evils had happened to him because he had been expected to live as a gentleman without proper means. In fact, he was the person who had been most injured. Her father, in his complete, in his almost abject tenderness towards her, could not say rough words in answer to all these arguments. He could only repeat his assertion over and over again that the man was utterly unworthy of her, and must be discarded. It was all as nothing. The man must discard himself.

"He is false as hell," said Sir Harry.

"And am I to be as false as hell also? Will you love me better when I have consented to be untrue? And even that would be a lie. I do love him. I must love him. I may be more wicked than he is, because I do so. But I do."

Poor Lady Elizabeth in these days was worse than useless. Her daughter was so strong that her weakness was as the weakness of water. She was driven hither and thither in a way that she herself felt to be disgraceful. When her husband told her that the cousin, as matter of course, could never be seen again, she assented. When Emily implored her to act as mediator with her father on behalf of the wicked cousin, she again assented. And then, when she was alone with Sir Harry, she did not dare to do as she had promised.

"I do think it will kill her," she said to Sir Harry.

"We must all die, but we need not die disgraced," he said.

It was a most solemn answer, and told the thoughts which had been dwelling in his mind. His son had gone from him; and now it might be that his daughter must go too, because she could not survive the disappointment of her young love. He had learned to think that it might be so as he looked at her great grave eyes, and her pale cheeks, and her sorrow-laden mouth. It might be so; but better that for them all than that she should be contaminated by the touch of a thing so vile as this cousin. She was pure as snow, clear as a star, lovely as the opening rosebud. As she was, let her go to her grave,—if it need be so. For himself, he could die too,—or even live if it were required of him! Other fathers, since Jephtha and Agamemnon, have recognised it as true that heaven has demanded from them their daughters.

The letter came, and was read and re-read by Sir Harry before he showed it to his child. He took it also to his wife, and explained it to her in all its points. "It has more craft," said he, "than I gave him credit for."

"I don't suppose he ever cared for her," said Lady Elizabeth.

"Nor for any human being that ever lived,—save himself. I wonder whether he got Boltby to write it for him."

"Surely Mr. Boltby wouldn't have done that."

"I don't know. I think he would do anything to rid us from what he believed to have been our danger. I don't think it was in George Hotspur to write such a letter out of his own head."

"But does it signify?"

"Not in the least. It is his own handwriting and his signature. Whoever formed the words, it is the same thing. It was needed only to prove to her that he had not even the merit of being true to her."

For a while Sir Harry thought that he would entrust to his wife the duty of showing the letter to Emily. He would so willingly have escaped the task himself! But as he considered the matter he feared that Lady Elizabeth might lack the firmness to explain the matter fully to the poor girl. The daughter would be so much stronger than the mother, and thus the thing that must be done would not be effected! At last, on the evening of the day on which the letter had reached him, he sent for her, and read it to her. She heard it without a word. Then he put it into her hands, and she read the sentences herself, slowly, one after another, endeavouring as she did so to find arguments by which she might stave off the conclusion to which she knew that her father would attempt to bring her.

"It must be all over now," said he at last.

She did not answer him, but gazed into his face with such a look of woe that his heart was melted. She had found no argument. There had not been in the whole letter one word of love for her.

"My darling, will it not be better that we should meet the blow?"

"I have met it, all along. Some day, perhaps, he might be different."

"In what way, dearest? He does not even profess to hope so himself."

"That gentleman in London, Papa, would have paid nothing for him unless he wrote like this. He had to do it. Papa, you had better just leave me to myself. I will not trouble you by mentioning his name."

"But Emily—"

"Well, Papa?"

"Mamma and I cannot bear that you should suffer alone."

"I must suffer, and silence is the easiest. I will go now and think about it. Dear Papa, I know that you have always done everything for the best."

He did not see her again that evening. Her mother was with her in her own room, and of course they were talking about Cousin George for hours together. It could not be avoided, in spite of what Emily had herself said of the expediency of silence. But she did not once allude to the possibility of a future marriage. As the man was so dear to her, and as he bore their name, and as he must inherit her father's title, could not some almost superhuman exertion be made for his salvation? Surely so much as that might be done, if they all made it the work of their lives.

"It must be the work of my life, Mamma," she said.

Lady Elizabeth forbore from telling her that there was no side on which she could approach him. The poor girl herself, however, must have felt that it was so. As she thought of it all she reminded herself that, though they were separated miles asunder, still she could pray for him. We need not doubt this at least,—that to him who utters them prayers of intercession are of avail.

On the following morning she was at breakfast, and both her father and mother remarked that something had been changed in her dress. The father only knew that it was so, but the mother could have told of every ribbon that had been dropped, and every ornament that had been laid aside. Emily Hotspur had lived a while, if not among the gayest of the gay, at least among the brightest of the bright in outside garniture, and having been asked to consult no questions of expense, had taught herself to dress as do the gay and bright and rich. Even when George had come on his last wretched visit to Humblethwaite, when she had known that he had been brought there as a blackamoor perhaps just capable of being washed white, she had not thought it necessary to lessen the gauds of her attire. Though she was saddened in her joy by the knowledge of the man's faults, she was still the rich daughter of a very wealthy man, and engaged to marry the future inheritor of all that wealth and riches. There was then no reason why she should lower her flag one inch before the world. But now all was changed with her! During the night she had thought of her apparel, and of what use it might be during her future life. She would never more go bright again, unless some miracle might prevail, and he still might be to her that which she had painted him. Neither father nor mother, as she kissed them both, said a word as to her appearance. They must take her away from Humblethwaite, change the scene, try to interest her in new pursuits; that was what they had determined to attempt. For the present, they would let her put on what clothes she pleased, and make no remark.

Early in the day she went out by herself. It was now December, but the weather was fine and dry, and she was for two hours alone, rambling through the park. She had made her attempt in life, and had failed. She owned her failure to herself absolutely. The image had no gold in it;—none as yet. But it was not as other images, which, as they are made, so must they remain to the end. The Divine Spirit, which might from the first have breathed into this clay some particle of its own worth, was still efficacious to bestow the gift. Prayer should not be wanting; but the thing as it now was she saw in all its impurity. He had never loved her. Had he loved her he would not have written words such as those she had read. He had pretended to love her in order that he might have money, that his debts might be paid, that he might not be ruined. "He hoped," he said in his letter, "he hoped that his cousin might be made happy by a splendid alliance!" She remembered well the abominable, heartless words. And this was the man who had pledged her to truth and firmness, and whose own truth and firmness she had never doubted for a moment, even when acknowledging to herself the necessity of her pledge to him. He had never loved her; and, though she did not say so, did not think so, she felt that of all his sins that sin was the one which could not be forgiven.

What should she now do with herself,—how bear herself at this present moment of her life? She did not tell herself now that she would die, though as she looked forward into life all was so dreary to her, that she would fain have known that death would give an escape. But there were duties for her still to do. During that winter ramble, she owned to herself for the first time that her father had been right in his judgment respecting their cousin, and that she, by her pertinacity, had driven her father on till on her account he had been forced into conduct which was distasteful to him. She must own to her father that he had been right; that the man, though she dearly loved him still, was of such nature that it would be quite unfit that she should marry him. There might still be the miracle; her prayers were still her own to give; of them she would say nothing to her father. She would simply confess to him that he had been right, and then beg of him to pardon her the trouble she had caused him.

"Papa," she said to him the following morning, "may I come to you?" She came in, and on this occasion sat down at his right hand. "Of course, you have been right, Papa," she said.

"We have both been right, dearest, I hope."

"No, Papa; I have been wrong! I thought I knew him, and I did not. I thought when you told me that he was so bad, that you were believing false people; and, Papa, I know now that I should not have loved him as I did;—so quickly, like that."

"Nobody has blamed you for a moment. Nobody has thought of blaming you."

"I blame myself enough; I can tell you that. I feel as though I had in a way destroyed myself."

"Do not say that, my darling."

"You will let me speak now; will you not, Papa? I wish to tell you everything, that you may understand all that I feel. I shall never get over it."

"You will, dearest; you will, indeed."

"Never! Perhaps I shall live on; but I feel that it has killed me for this world. I don't know how a girl is to get over it when she has said that she has loved any one. If they are married, then she does not want to get over it; but if they are not,—if he deserts her, or is unworthy, or both,—what can she do then, but just go on thinking of it till—she dies?"

Sir Harry used with her all the old accustomed arguments to drive such thoughts out of her head. He told her how good was God to His creatures, and, specially, how good in curing by the soft hand of time such wounds as those from which she was suffering. She should "retrick her beams," and once more "flame in the forehead of the morning sky," if only she would help the work of time by her own endeavours. "Fight against the feeling, Emily, and try to conquer it, and it will be conquered."

"But, Papa, I do not wish to conquer it. I should not tell you of all this, only for one thing."

"What thing, dearest?"

"I am not like other girls, who can just leave themselves alone and be of no trouble. You told me that if I outlived you—"

"The property will be yours; certainly. Of course, it was my hope,—and is,—that all that shall be settled by your marriage before my death. The trouble and labour is more than a woman should be called on to support alone."

"Just so. And it is because you are thinking of all this, that I feel it right to tell you. Papa, I shall never be married."

"We will leave that for the present, Emily."

"Very well; only if it would make a change in your will, you should make it. You will have to be here, Papa, after I am gone,—probably."

"No, no, no."

"But, if it were not so, I should not know what to do. That is all, Papa; only this,—that I beg your pardon for all the trouble I have caused you." Then she knelt before him, and he kissed her head, and blessed her, and wept over her.

There was nothing more heard from Cousin George at Humblethwaite, and nothing more heard of him for a long time. Mr. Boltby did pay his debts, having some terribly hard struggles with Mr. Hart and Captain Stubber before the liquidations were satisfactorily effected. It was very hard to make Mr. Hart and Captain Stubber understand that the Baronet was paying these debts simply because he had said that he would pay them once before, under other circumstances, and that no other cause for their actual payment now existed. But the debts were paid, down to the last farthing of which Mr. Boltby could have credible tidings. "Pay everything," Sir Harry had said; "I have promised it." Whereby he was alluding to the promise which he had made to his daughter. Everything was paid, and

Cousin George was able to walk in and out of his club, a free man,—and at times almost happy,—with an annuity of five hundred pounds a year! Nothing more was said to him as to the necessity of expatriation.

Chapter XXIV.

The End.

Among playgoing folk, in the following April there was a great deal of talk about the marriage of that very favourite actress, Mrs. Morton. She appeared in the playbills as Mrs. George Hotspur, late Mrs. Morton. Very many spoke of her familiarly, who knew her only on the stage,—as is the custom of men in speaking of actresses,—and perhaps some few of these who spoke of her did know her personally. "Poor Lucy!" said one middle-aged gentleman over fifty, who spent four nights of every week at one theatre or another. "When she was little more than a child they married her to that reprobate Morton. Since that she has managed to keep her head above water by hard work; and now she has gone and married another worse than the first!"

"She is older now, and will be able to manage George," said another.

"Manage him! If anybody can manage to keep him out of debt, or from drink either, I'll eat him."

"But he must be Sir George when old Sir Harry dies," said he who was defending the prudence of the marriage.

"Yes, and won't have a penny. Will it help her to be able to put Lady Hotspur on the bills? Not in the least. And the women can't forgive her and visit her. She has not been good enough for that. A grand old family has been disgraced, and a good actress destroyed. That's my idea of this marriage."

"I thought Georgy was going to marry his cousin—that awfully proud minx," said one young fellow.

"When it came to the scratch, she would not have him," said another. "But there had been promises, and so, to make it all square, Sir Harry paid his debts."

"I don't believe a bit about his debts being paid," said the middle-aged gentleman who was fond of going to the theatre.

Yes, George Hotspur was married: and, as far as any love went with him, had married the woman he liked best. Though the actress was worlds too good for him, there was not about her that air of cleanliness and almost severe purity which had so distressed him while he had been forced to move in the atmosphere of his cousin. After the copying of the letter and the settlement of the bills, Mrs. Morton had found no difficulty in arranging matters as she pleased. She had known the man perhaps better than any one else had known him; and yet she thought it best to marry him. We must not inquire into her motives, though we may pity her fate.

She did not intend, however, to yield herself as an easy prey to his selfishness. She had also her ideas of reforming him, and ideas which, as they were much less grand, might possibly be more serviceable than those which for a while had filled the mind and heart of Emily Hotspur. "George," she said, one day to him, "what do you mean to do?" This was before the marriage was fixed;—when nothing more was fixed than that idea of marriage which had long existed between them.

"Of course we shall be spliced now," said he.

"And if so, what then? I shall keep to the stage, of course."

"We couldn't do with the £500 a year, I suppose, any how?"

"Not very well, I'm afraid, seeing that as a habit you eat and drink more than that yourself. But, with all that I can do, there must be a change. I tell you for your own sake as well as for mine, unless you can drop drinking, we had better give it up even yet." After that, for a month or two under her auspices, he did "drop it,"—or at least so far dropped it as to induce her to run the risk. In April they were married, and she must be added to the list of women who have sacrificed themselves on behalf of men whom they have known to be worthless. We need not pursue his career further; but we may be sure, that though she watched him very closely, and used a power over him of which he was afraid, still he went gradually from bad to worse, and was found at last to be utterly past redemption. He was one who in early life had never known what it was to take delight in postponing himself to another; and now there was no spark in him of love or gratitude by which fire could be kindled or warmth created. It had come to that with him,—that to eat and to drink was all that was left to him; and it was coming to that too, that the latter of these two pleasant recreations would soon be all that he had within his power of enjoyment. There are such men; and of all human beings they are the most to be pitied. They have intellects; they do think; the hours with them are terribly long;—and they have no hope!

The Hotspurs of Humblethwaite remained at home till Christmas was passed, and then at once started for Rome. Sir Harry and Lady Elizabeth both felt that it must be infinitely better for their girl to be away; and then there came the doctor's slow advice. There was nothing radically amiss with Miss Hotspur, the doctor said; but it would be better for her to be taken elsewhere. She, knowing how her father loved his home and the people around him, begged that she might be allowed to stay. Nothing ailed her, she said, save only that ache at the heart which no journey to Rome could cure. "What's the use of it, Papa?" she said. "You are unhappy because I'm altered. Would you wish me not to be altered after what has passed? Of course I am altered. Let us take it as it is, and not think about it." She had adopted certain practices in life, however, which Sir Harry was determined to check, at any rate for the time. She spent her days among the poor, and when not with them she was at church. And there was always some dreary book in her hands when they were together in the drawing-room after dinner. Of church-going and visiting the poor, and of good books, Sir Harry approved thoroughly; but even of good things such as these there may be too much. So Sir Harry and Lady Elizabeth got a courier who spoke all languages, and a footman who spoke German, and two maids, of whom one pretended to speak French, and had trunks packed without number, and started for Rome. All that wealth could do was done; but let the horseman be ever so rich, or the horseman's daughter, and the stud be ever so good, it is seldom they can ride fast enough to shake off their cares.

In Rome they remained till April, and while they were there the name of Cousin George was never once mentioned in the hearing of Sir Harry. Between the mother and daughter no doubt there was speech concerning him. But to Emily's mind he was always present. He was to her as a thing abominable, and yet necessarily tied to her by bonds which she could never burst asunder. She felt like some poor princess in a tale, married to an ogre from whom there was no escape. She had given herself up to one utterly worthless, and she knew it. But yet she had given herself, and could not revoke the gift. There was, indeed, still left to her that possibility of a miracle, but of that she whispered nothing even to her mother. If there were to be a miracle, it must be of God; and at God's throne she made her whispers. In these days she was taken about from sight to sight with apparent willingness. She saw churches, pictures, statues, and ruins, and seemed to take an interest in them. She was introduced to the Pope, and allowed herself to be apparelled in her very best for that august occasion. But, nevertheless, the tenor of her way and the fashions of her life, as was her daily dress, were grey and sad and solemn. She lived as one who knew that the backbone of her life was broken. Early in April they left Rome and went north, to the Italian lakes, and settled themselves for a while at Lugano. And here the news reached them of the marriage of George Hotspur.

Lady Elizabeth read the marriage among the advertisements in the *Times*, and at once took it to Sir Harry, withdrawing the paper from the room in a manner which made Emily sure that there was something in it which she was not intended to see. But Sir Harry thought that the news should be told to her, and he himself told it.

"Already married!" she said. "And who is the lady?"

"You had better not ask, my dear."

"Why not ask? I may, at any rate, know her name."

"Mrs. Morton. She was a widow,—and an actress."

"Oh yes, I know," said Emily, blushing; for in those days in which it had been sought to wean her from George Hotspur, a word or two about this lady had been said to her by Lady Elizabeth under the instructions of Sir Harry. And there was no more said on that occasion. On that day, and on the following, her father observed no change in her; and the mother spoke nothing of her fears. But on the next morning Lady Elizabeth said that she was not as she had been. "She is thinking of him still—always," she whispered to her husband. He made no reply, but sat alone, out in the garden, with his newspaper before him, reading nothing, but cursing that cousin of his in his heart.

There could be no miracle now for her! Even the thought of that was gone. The man who had made her believe that he loved her, only in the last autumn,—though indeed it seemed to her that years had rolled over since, and made her old, worn-out, and weary;—who had asked for and obtained the one gift she had to give, the bestowal of her very self; who had made her in her baby folly believe that he was almost divine, whereas he was hardly human in his lowness,—this man, whom she still loved in a way which she could not herself understand, loving and despising him utterly at the same time,—was now the husband of another woman. Even he, she had felt, would have thought something of her. But she had been nothing to him but the means of escape from disreputable difficulties. She could not sustain her contempt for herself as she remembered this, and yet she showed but little of it in her outward manner.

"I'll go when you like, Papa," she said when the days of May had come, "but I'd sooner stay here a little longer if you wouldn't mind." There was no talk of going home. It was only a question whether they should go further north, to Lucerne, before the warm weather came.

"Of course we will remain; why not?" said Sir Harry. "Mamma and I like Lugano amazingly." Poor Sir Harry. As though he could have liked any place except Humblethwaite!

Our story is over now. They did remain till the scorching July sun had passed over their heads, and August was upon them; and then—they had buried her in the small Protestant cemetery at Lugano, and Sir Harry Hotspur was without a child and without an heir.

He returned home in the early autumn, a grey, worn-out, tottering old man, with large eyes full of sorrow, and a thin mouth that was seldom opened to utter a word. In these days, I think, he recurred to his early sorrow, and thought almost more of his son than of his daughter. But he had instant, pressing energy left to him for one deed. Were he to die now without a further will, Humblethwaite and Scarrowby would go to the wretch who had destroyed him. What was the title to him now, or even the name? His wife's nephew was an Earl with an enormous rent-roll, something so large that Humblethwaite and Scarrowby to him would be little more than additional labour. But to this young man Humblethwaite and Scarrowby were left, and the glories of the House of Hotspur were at an end.

And so the story of the House of Humblethwaite has been told.

THE END

Books in beautiful packages...

Norilana Books
Classics

www.norilana.com

Publishing some of the best, rare, and precious classics of world literature in trade hardcover and paperback editions.

Lightning Source UK Ltd.
Milton Keynes UK
06 January 2011
165268UK00001B/194/P